Cellar Door

Jackson Arthur

I dedicate this to all of those who have loved and supported me, through both the darkness and the light.

VELOX BOOKS
Published by arrangement with the author.

Cellar Door copyright © 2022 by Jackson Arthur.

All Rights Reserved.

This book is a work of fiction. People, places, events, and situations are the product of the author's imagination. Any resemblance to actual persons, living or dead, or historical events, is purely coincidental.

No part of this book may be reproduced, stored in a retrieval system, or transmitted by any means without the written permission of the author and publisher.

"[The neurotic] feels caught in a **cellar** with many **doors**, and whichever **door** he opens leads only into new darkness. And all the time he knows that others are walking outside in sunshine."
—Karen Horney

"Most English-speaking people… will admit that **cellar door** is 'beautiful', especially if dissociated from its sense (and from its spelling). … More beautiful than, say, sky, and far more beautiful than beautiful."
—J.R.R. Tolkien

CONTENTS

The Unexpected Friend _____ 1

Dorothy (She Ran up the Stairs) _____ 16

Evolution Inc. _____ 28

Black Ice _____ 44

I Dreamed of Monsters _____ 56

The Devil Down Below _____ 84

Jupiter Street _____ 92

Awake into a Dream _____ 95

Shackled and Chained _____ 112

About the Author _____ 124

THE UNEXPECTED FRIEND

THIS EVENING, LIKE most of the evenings over the past five years, Sky is traveling an all too familiar route toward Orwell Ohio, a nothing little town where one could spot as many Amish buggies as motor vehicles on the road. In that nothing town, like a lot of nothing towns in Northeastern Ohio, there is a large factory.

And like most people that live in Northeastern Ohio, Sky is a factory worker. Living the American dream. For the third week in a row, her bosses are forcing her into yet another mandatory weekend.

She is ready for a day off. She needs it, like she needs oxygen.

For the love of whatever god or devil might be looking out for the factory workers of Ohio, she is beyond ready for a night of camping and drinking and carrying on.

Sky groans quietly, before deciding to suck it up.

"What was that?" a voice asks from the passenger seat.

Sky glances at Bethany. The fading sun pierces the windshield and casts a bar of light at the top of Bethany's head, which bears a slight resemblance to either a halo or a crown.

"Huh?" Sky replies.

"You sighed."

"I did not," Sky says and then giggles.

"You totally sighed just now," Bethany responds, before giggling too. "I'm just busting your balls. I get it. I feel the same. Another Saturday night in that shit hole is too freaking much."

"I want to go camping so bad," Sky states. "You camp?"

"Sleep on the ground?" Bethany replies. "Pass."

"Trust me. You won't mind the ground," Sky says, "because you will be way too drunk to feel anything by then."

"Truth," Bethany replies. "I'll still pass on that, though. I do wish we were going somewhere else, though. Bar. Club. Strip club. Key West. Anywhere but back to flippin' work for the thousandth time. *Blows*. At least Steve is going to be the floor supervisor."

Sky gives Bethany another swift glance, her eyes bugging out of her head. "Right! He is soooo sexy!"

"Yes, he is," Bethany replies. "He can supervise my floor anytime. Along with my couch, my bed, and my shower… and my countertops while he is at it."

Nodding along, Sky adds, "Yea. Mr. Fine can even supervise the backseat of *this car* if he wanted."

Bethany responds with another giggle before exploding into full roaring laughter. "I might just have to carpool with you on that shit, too. You know? Bang. Bang. Bang."

"Gross!" Sky cries out. "You're gonna have to wait your turn. Nasty girl."

Bethany is petite, with smooth, pale skin. Her dark black hair naturally forms curls that are both bouncy and playful. The smooth skin of Bethany's youthful face is spotted by clusters of tiny freckles. In Sky's opinion,

Bethany resembles an old-time, classic style porcelain doll, similar to the type that Sky's Na-Na used to collect.

Along with resembling a porcelain doll, Bethany also speaks with a squeaky, child-like voice.

Bethany's appearance gives the misleading illusion that she is sweet, innocent, and perhaps a little naïve. Sky had almost bought into the illusion, at first. Yet, after getting to know Bethany, she recognized that the resemblance of being child-like and sweet went only skin deep. It is an unintentional mask that Bethany is forced to wear. Bethany is perverted, blunt, honest, loud, far from innocent, and absolutely hilarious. And after three months of carpooling, Sky is no longer a bit surprised by any of the dirty things that often spill from Bethany's lips.

And it always makes the often grueling ride to work into something somewhat bearable.

"How did I ever get stuck riding with your bitch ass every single day?" Sky asks.

"Could be fate. Could be luck," Bethany replies. "Or it could be a plot to abduct and sell your firm ass as a sex slave that has gone on waaaayyyy too long. Only God knows that shit."

"Truth!" Sky agrees. "Or it could be that your dumb ass truck broke down on your second day and I took pity on your sorry, broke behind enough to swoop to the rescue. Because I am selfless and awesome, like a superhero. Like I'm the Supergirl of Northeastern Ohio. Or maybe Wonder Woman. Or some other awesome heroine who wears spandex outside no matter the season. Or something…"

Bethany nods, "Or something."

"But luckily for you," Sky adds, "you also just happen to live in the same town as me. And I just happen to go right by your apartment on my way. Or else you might have been screwed. I mean. I might be totally selfless and heroic, but I really hate backtracking. You know?"

"*Same,*" Bethany replies.

"Hell yea!" Sky suddenly blurts. "I love this song." Quickly, she removes a hand from the wheel and boosts the volume on her Sirius radio up a few notches. The opening chords to *Melissa* begin. Not only does she hum along with the sad, crying guitars, but Sky also launches into vocals, singing along with the first verse.

"*Crossroads… seem to come and go…*"

Not long after upgrading her Honda's standard stereo system to satellite radio, Sky discovered a station titled *Crossroads,* a channel entirely dedicated to the Allman Brothers Band and other similar classic rock bands.

It was like winning the lottery.

Classic rock and roll, especially The Allman Brothers Band, always reminds Sky of camping. Her childhood. And her father.

As the final notes of the song play, Sky reaches to turn the music back down. She is suddenly halted by an unexpected explosion of terrible sound, an onslaught of vicious static that savagely erupts throughout the speakers.

The wicked detonation draws a startled shriek from Bethany.

For several seconds, the sharp clamor slices and cuts at Sky's brain. She fights to connect her scattered thoughts. Somehow, she manages to piece together one clear and obvious question.

"Can satellite radios even get static?"

Just when Sky is certain that the bones of her skull are about to shatter beneath the white noise that beats against them, the static stops. She manages to loosen a lung full of air, unsure at what point she began holding her breath.

The following silence is like a glimpse of Heaven. But it is short-lived. Sky expects her radio to return to normal and loud music to resume, but that does not happen. Instead, something happens that confuses Sky even more.

A single man, a single resounding voice, firing off urgent words like thundering gunshots, bombarding the speakers at a rapid pace.

"Please don't turn me off," the man says. "Please. You need to listen."

Beneath the words, Sky can easily identify stress and desperation in the man's voice. She brings the volume down to a reasonable tone, but for some reason does not switch stations or turn the radio off.

She glances at Bethany, wondering if her passenger is feeling the same confusion.

Meeting Sky's gaze, Bethany asks, "Is he a DJ?"

"Sirius radio wouldn't have a DJ," Sky reminds Bethany. "Remember? It only has music. That's why I have to pay $10 a month."

"Who is he then?"

"I have no clue."

"It hasn't begun yet," the man says. "The invasion has. But not the war. Not yet. We still have time. But not much, I'm afraid."

The frantic man continues.

"So, I need to be quick. As children, we were taught, all of us, to be wary of strangers. Don't talk to them. They will hurt us. Wrong! We have been wrong the whole time. We have been afraid of the wrong people. It won't be strangers that get us…"

"What a psycho," Bethany states, before asking Sky to change the station.

"... Invasion never happens like in movies..."

"Right," Sky agrees. "I don't know why people buy into this conspiracy bullshit."

"... There won't be any grand invading force..."

"Yea," Bethany replies. "What a loser."

"... That is not how it will happen..."

"Please turn off this garbage," Bethany asks again, gradually growing more aggressive each time. *"It is giving me a headache."*

Sky continues to ignore her requests, though, as the man drones on. "It will not come in the form of an approaching army at our gates, because the enemy will not be using brute, blunt force. They are smarter than that. And... the invasion is already happening. Look all around you. The nice new couple that recently moved into the neighborhood two houses down from you. The new handsome or cute employee at your job. The beautiful girl at the local Shop n Save who begins to flirt back. The unexpected friend..."

New couple. Cute employee. What? What does that even mean? Sky wonders. An unexpected friend? Most friends are unexpected to a point. That could mean anything. Anyone. Unexpected friend? It could even mean someone like... Bethany?

The voice continues, "I am not crazy. The invasion has already begun. It's too late to go back and stop it now. The clock is winding down, but it has not reached Zero Hour yet..."

Zero Hour?

"... Right under our noses, in plain sight, the enemies have been making their moves. Slowly sliding their pieces into place over the past... I'm not entirely sure how long. Too long. And they are not only infiltrating places of power, they are also causally inserting themselves into the lives of everyday people. Like you. Into your neighborhoods. Into your jobs. Into your inner circles. In time, they will be everywhere. And when the time comes to strike, there will be no stopping them. It's a drawn-out strategy from a very patient foe. By very slowly tightening their grasp around us, we would remain blind and oblivious to the fact the enemy had grabbed onto us until our life is suddenly squeezed away…"

"I'll just turn the shit off myself!" Bethany exclaims as she reaches for the radio's power button.

"… And it would have worked, too…."

Mindless reaction causes Sky to slap Bethany's hand away, drawing a startled cry of outrage.

"What is your problem?" Sky asks.

"What the fuck is *your* problem?"

"Why do you want me to turn it off so bad?" Sky demands. "You are acting weird! Why can't you just chill out!?"

"… But their entire plan hinged on one thing, the ability to move unseen until everything is in place…"

Something nags at Sky from the back of her mind, something that she is obviously missing.

But what?

"… They slipped up," the strange man continues.

With his next words, Sky witnesses the man's voice taking on a new quality, a new tone, one seemingly on the edge of pure insanity.

"… And now I can see them…"

Unlike the previous attempt, Bethany does not speak or give Sky any warning before she lunges her hand toward the console of the radio. Sky again reacts, slapping at Bethany's moving arm. But this time, Sky is unable to react fast enough to keep Bethany's finger from hitting its target.

The button is pushed. The radio channel changes. But it doesn't matter. Because the single voice follows them. Bethany pushes the button again and again and again, but the man's voice is everywhere.

This places the final piece into the puzzle. Sky asks aloud, "If this is just some nutjob, how the hell would he be able to hijack my satellite radio?"

As if answering Sky's question, "… I am using satellites and the internet to send my message across the globe. Televisions. Smartphones. Smart tablets. Video game systems. Streaming services like Hulu or Netflix. XM radio. I will send myself as far as the reaches of our technology will take me. Anywhere I can get the word out. Some of you are hearing my voice. Some of you can see my face. I don't know how long I will be able to continue reaching you before they silence me. I am… afraid, but I will no longer hide. My name is Dr. Wesley Brant, and I am trying to save you all…"

Is this even possible?

Sky then notices a set of bright headlights from an approaching vehicle, heading their direction along the opposite lane. As the dark SUV passes them, she wonders if the same strange man is speaking to them, too.

Bethany desperately pounds down on the station button several more times, but Dr. Brant speaks out from every channel, like a preacher spouting scripture from an altar that is raised high and far from reach.

Sky takes her eyes from the road and glances at Bethany. Why is she acting so strange right now? Sky questions. Acting… a little… erratic. Why is she so desperate to shut off Dr. Brant?

"… I have seen our invaders," Dr. Brant goes on. "And they are cunning and clever. They do not have the strength to attack with brute force. So instead, they are using the shadows and our own tunnel vision against us.

They are dangerous. But they are also weak and cowardly. And they have chosen to move behind our backs instead of meeting us face-to-face. But not any longer…"

As Sky is looking at Bethany, something bewildering happens. At first, Sky is unsure whether it is real, but Bethany seems to alter, to change in some bizarre way. The change does not happen physically. And, if she were later asked to do so, Sky would find it near impossible to describe this change in words.

"I have seen them," Dr. Brant insists. "And I need you to see them too. Open your eyes and listen to my words. Look with an open mind. The invaders are all around you. Once everyone else, the rest of you around the world, sees them, too, we can then begin to fight…"

If Sky had to explain this change to another person, it would be like this. Across the surface of Bethany's pale, porcelain-like exterior, thin, metaphorical fissures begin to crack apart and spread. As the fissures become wide, gaping crevasses, Sky is able to see below the disguise. Then, as Bethany's shell crumbles away, Sky is no longer looking at the same person that has been her carpooling buddy for the past few months.

"… You must…"

Sky has always known that Bethany's innocent, doll-like appearance isn't true to the person beneath it. Just like how a beautiful, precious puppy will chew your favorite shoes, rip up the trash, and piss all over the furniture the minute no one is watching.

But, as the outer shell of her friend falls away, Sky is left with something truly… unexpected.

"… Can you see them?"

A complete stranger.

"… Can you see them?"

A silent invader?

As Sky stares at Bethany, she realizes that Bethany is staring back. Their eyes meet and something passes unseen between them. Without warning, Bethany reaches over and grabs hold of the steering wheel. A brief tug-of-war for control over the vehicle ends with the Honda sharply swerving, violently lunging over the white edge line and off the road.

From the blackness of the night, a broad tree materializes directly in their path. Headlights spill across the surface of the thick trunk, forming large glowing orbs. Somehow, Sky manages to find the brake with her left foot. Thrusting down onto the pedal with as much force as her leg muscles are capable of, Sky fails to keep the Honda from wrapping around the solid base of the tall tree.

During the collision, Sky nearly blacks out. Visually everything falls away, a total eclipse of her sight. Her other senses, however, fully experience the two seconds that take place between the instant her car smashes into the tree and the moment when it succumbs to the undeniably violent stop.

Metal savagely twists, bends, and implodes as the front-end hammers home. Sky's seat belt, which had been buckled out of habit, instantaneously tightens its grip on her.

Lungs deflate.

And ribs fracture.

The windshield disintegrates in a clasp of thunder, before slivers of glass rain across her like sharp hail.

A massive *crash* fills her ears, like the detonation of a grenade, when her airbag inflates. Hitting the airbag feels more like hitting the side of a brick wall. The cartilage of her nose bends and nearly caves in, but somehow keeps from snapping. And her neck pops from bottom to top, luckily without breaking.

Sky doesn't have time to be paralyzed by pain, though. She needs to act. She needs to move. But the first thing that she needs to do is catch her breath, no matter how damaged her ribs are or how much oxygen feels like razors.

Her eyes shoot open.

Instincts scream for her to get out of the car.

Run! Run!

However, when Sky shifts her body toward the door, the locked seat belt restricts her movements. Reaching down, she tries to disengage it, but during the collision, the latch somehow jammed. Like Bethany with the buttons on the radio, Sky jabs at it with her thumb over and over and over, but the belt won't release. Claustrophobia threatens to squeeze away her will power, as she frantically fights to free herself from the simple contraption.

Right when Sky borders on insanity, she remembers that her utility knife is in the front right pocket of her khaki pants. The razor is worn and mostly dulled from work, but it should be sharp enough to cut through the seat belt. Sky pulls the knife free, but then hears coughing and hacking from the passenger seat.

Somehow, in her frenzy to get loose, Sky forgot about Bethany, who appears to be returning to consciousness. The two girls suddenly lock eyes. Like a leaping python, Bethany instantly lunges toward Sky. Bethany never wanted to wear her seat belt, no matter how much Sky lectured her. But that lack of restraint provides Bethany enough mobility to wrap Sky in a firm headlock.

Sky frantically digs her stubby fingernails into the flesh of her attacker's arms, struggling violently and fiercely against her narrowing airway. She forces herself to inhale as hard and as deeply as possible, taking in whatever wisps of air that she might squeeze down her throat before it closes completely. Faint, lingering smoke slides into her lungs, along with drops of blood from her bleeding nose, which burns her airway, causing her to gasp and choke.

"Why are you doing this?" Sky whispers. "Please, just…"

Sky is unsure whether or not Bethany hears her low raspy pleads, because she doesn't receive an answer.

Instead, Bethany shouts, "You need to quit! You need to just quit this shit!"

But Sky isn't quitting. She is going to fight back, like Dr. Brant says. Swiftly, Sky throws her fists and elbows at Bethany, hoping that one good hit might loosen the hold on her throat. But the attacks are awkward and make little difference.

Bethany clumsily jerks at Sky's upper body as she tries to pull Sky over to her own seat, most likely to gain better leverage. But luckily the seat belt remains jammed and locked and refuses to let go of Sky, like the incorruptible hug of a guardian angel.

Abruptly, Sky halts her arms from their mindless flailing. She forces a shallow, agony and blood-filled breath in order to regain her mental composure. Panic has clouded her mind. And she has forgotten about her utility knife, which she still grasps.

With a push of her thumb, the blade slides free.

Ferociously, Sky thrusts the exposed blade toward Bethany's leg. The razor is worn and dull, yet it sinks effortlessly into Bethany's flesh. At once, a bubble of dark blood rises from the wound, and then quickly flows down Bethany's leg in a narrow stream.

A wounded leg does not stop Bethany. Rather than reestablishing the same tight hold, Bethany pulls away her right arm, leaving only a single left arm wrapped around Sky's throat. The hold is loose, slightly weaker, but with her free arm, Bethany begins an awkward attempt at seizing the utility knife from Sky's grasp.

Grabbing and smacking. Tugging and tearing. Jerking and wrenching. Pulling. Pulling. And pulling. Sky does everything in her power to keep Bethany from getting a finger on the weapon. Yet, because Bethany has the upper hand, Sky is outmatched and overpowered.

She needs to fight smarter.

Sky slows the hand holding the razor knife and allows Bethany to loosely wrap fingers around her wrist. While Bethany pulls on Sky's arm, Sky gathers what little vigor she has left.

Passionately, Sky screams through a wide, gaping mouth, as she grabs hold of her own arm with her free hand. Using not just the muscles of her arms, but those of her upper body, her shoulders and back, Sky pulls upward, toward her chest, toward her aching lungs, toward her center of gravity.

Surprisingly, Sky's tired arms are able to bring the knife level to her heart. She pulls and pulls until she simply can't pull any further. And then, without warning, Sky pushes. Caught off guard by the unexpected shift in momentum, Bethany is helpless to stop the blade of the utility knife from plunging squarely into the middle of her chest.

Before Bethany has the chance to recover, Sky stabs her several more times in the upper body. Silent shock and rushing death fill Bethany's face, making her unable to speak or cry out.

Sky doesn't bother to wipe away the sticky layer of blood coating the razor blade. Instead, she finally frees herself from the seat belt. After forcing open the battered car door, Sky fumbles out in an exhausted and beaten heap. As the river of adrenaline pumping and pounding through her veins dries up, the simple desire to survive keeps Sky moving, rather than folding into a fetal position.

Somehow, Sky manages to rise to her feet. Glancing at the crushed and disfigured chunk of metal that had once been her Honda, Sky fights the urge to vomit.

Turning from rubble, she slowly stumbles and crosses the handful of yards dividing her crushed car and the side of the two-lane road. The full moon, hanging in the clear sky, pours down unhindered beams of light. By that light, Sky can see that she is standing at the edge of a dense and shadowy stretch of woods.

On the opposite side of the road is a massive, open field. The piece of land is obviously familiar to Sky, after having driven by it on a thousand different occasions while on her way to work. A white, three-story house sits to the left of the open field. Even though the house is a hundred or so yards back from the road, the large, looming structure, and its adjacent red barn, can easily be seen from the road.

In the mornings, Sky would sometimes see the Amish family that lives there. Children running and playing. Plain women gardening or hanging laundry. Strong men tending and farming the field.

The familiarity of her surroundings places much needed ground beneath Sky's feet. She no longer feels like she is free-falling.

From the direction of the Amish farm, Sky detects faint voices in the air. She then notices orbs of light, possibly flashlights, moving in a group toward her.

They must have heard the crash.

The sight of the approaching Amish family suddenly fills Sky with a harrowing sense of dread and the frantic urgency of purpose. Dr. Brant explained that he had hijacked satellites and the internet in order to warn people. But the Amish, even the more evolved families, don't generally use devices, like smartphones or televisions that are connected to the internet. Or radio systems that are linked to satellites. Or anything else of that nature.

They have no idea what is going on. Their world is no longer the same. And they need to know. The invasion. The secret war. They need to know about all of it.

Is it up to her to warn them? Sky wonders. Like Dr. Brant, has the burden fallen onto her shoulders as well?

Sky has always believed that there would be plenty of time for tents and camping and cold beer and menthol cigarettes and the Allman Brothers. She is young. Has a long life ahead of her. But she has been wrong all along. She was never aware that the clock had been counting down the entire time. And now, in the blink of an eye, the clock has reached Zero Hour.

As Sky hobbles, painfully jogging across the road and toward the approaching lights, questions shout from the very back parts of her mind. What if these people already know what is happening, somehow? What if they know because they are also silent invaders, like Bethany?

Sky tightens her grasp on the utility knife she still holds and continues forward.

DOROTHY (SHE RAN UP THE STAIRS)

THE PLACE WAS like a mansion.

That was the first thought I remember having when my mother, father, and I moved into the two-story house on Greenmeadow Drive. Looking back, I know that the house had been far from a movie star quality home, but my world was much smaller back then. I was eight years old at the time and had only lived in a tiny two-bedroom apartment downtown before moving into the country. That new house was a drastic change in my world, going from a hole-in-the-wall to a real, actual home.

It was like apples and oranges, to my young brain.

And there was so much open space outside. I was no longer living in a cramped city where everyone was piled on top of each other, suffocating. I never had a yard before, either, especially not one that seemed to go on forever. I had only seen such things in movies or on television. And when I stood in our new front yard and looked around, all I could see was open land and far-off woods.

No other people.

No other house.

Nothing but *my family* for *miles*.

I was a king, and this would be my new kingdom.

I clearly remember the day we moved in. It was hectic. We honestly didn't have a whole lot of stuff to pack and move, but the little we did seemed to take forever to get situated. As an energetic young boy, my feet were itching to run and explore all the new places available to me.

I wasn't allowed to just dart off, however.

Not right away, at least.

"This is your new home, too," I recall my dad telling me. "Grab whatever your little arms can carry and hustle. We need to have your room ready enough to spend the night."

Geesh.

For a little boy with zero patience, it was the longest, best day ever.

Whenever I think about the house on Greenmeadow, I always call it the Red House, because of the red paint that covered the exterior, which had been worn and peeling in spots. I have never figured out what possessed the previous owners of the house to paint it a barnyard-red, but that color always stood out in my memory.

When we finally got done for the day, the sun was low, the air was cool, and I had just enough light left to play outside for one whole hour. And for one complete hour, I never stopped moving, not even for a second.

And it was glorious.

***

The first few days at the Red House were brilliant.

I never spent so much time outside.

I battled imaginary armies. I searched for hidden treasures. Dragons and dark elves and evil wizards were all around me. I even saved a princess or two from peril.

In truth, all I did was run around, screaming and yelling at the tip-top of my lungs, because there was no one else within earshot of my ruckus. Only the birds and bees and whatever furry creatures might be hiding in the far-off woods.

It was the purest form of freedom.

However, my leash had only been so long, and my mom had to pull it taught quite often, as could be expected. I was only allowed to go so far from the house, and I had to remain within shouting distance at all times.

Whenever it was lunchtime, dinnertime, or the light of the day fell away, my mom would walk onto the front porch and yell at the top of her lungs, "Little Shane! Are you dead yet!? You better come in before the pack of wild dogs gets you!"

My mom had the weirdest sense of humor.

She still does.

Looking back, I fully understand my short leash and frustrating boundaries. Having two kids of my own now, I wouldn't have given my son and daughter that long of a rope, even in the open country. The thought of what could have happened makes my heart beat faster and my pulse quicken.

But things were different back then, or at least that is what I am always told.

I had so much fun those first few days, but when you're eight years old, you can only run around the same area so long before it starts to get repetitive.

We no longer lived in the city, but my dad still had to work there. It was a long commute and my dad often worked long days, which meant that he wasn't around a lot. Whenever I have memories of living in the Red

House, he is rarely in them. It is usually just my mom and me. The few memories I do have of him normally involve him either coming or going.

After quickly growing bored outside, I eventually moved my curiosities and wanderings indoors.

Thinking back, it's kind of funny.

The great outdoors had seemed so appealing, at the time, so mysterious. There were so many new, exciting things to discover there, or so I had thought. I would never have predicted that all along there had been something mysterious, and even frightening, waiting for me within the four walls of our new home.

***

The bottom floor of the Red House consisted of the front foyer, living room, dining room, kitchen, large closet, and half-bath. Everything flowed in a circular pattern, one room connected to the next, which was then open to the next. Around and around. At the center of the circle were the stairs that led to the three bedrooms and single bathroom on the second floor.

Once inside, I rummaged through every dusty nook and shadowy cranny that I could find, hoping to find some secret passage or hidden portal to another world. But all I eventually found was more boredom.

And a little loneliness.

Not even a week into living at the Red House, and I was already regretting it.

The new car smell had worn off too quickly.

It wasn't long before I was missing the hustle and bustle of the active city, where there was always something to do and other people around. All that new open space suddenly felt... empty.

I can recall the day that I met Dorothy with absolute clarity.

I had been sitting on the very bottom step of the stairs, bored and thinking about my friend Taj. Taj had lived in the city, too, in the same building as my family, just two floors up. There had been a small community playground in the back lot of the building. It had a swing-set, a tall slide, and a large sandbox. Taj's mother and my own mom would often take us both to play while they chatted it up on a nearby bench.

As I sat there on the stairs that day, my eyes closed as tight as possible, I was listening to Taj's voice in my head. I was feeling the swings going up and down, up and down. I was remembering how it felt to have clumpy sand between my toes. I was missing my best friend and wanting to go home.

But something then broke into those memories and dragged me out.

The sound of giggling.

Was my mom playing a joke on me?

I remember that being my first thought whenever I began hearing the strange giggling. I immediately pictured my mother hiding somewhere and waiting for me to come find her. She would use the giggling to lure me in. And then she would jump out from around a corner or from behind something to scare me.

We would both laugh.

Or at least that was what I pictured when the giggling had started.

But it only took a second or two to realize that the giggling could not have been my mother, because it was too tiny, obviously from someone much younger. And my dad was in the city, as usual, so it couldn't have been him, either.

It almost sounded like a young child.

Possibly a little girl.

I climbed down the stairs and began to follow the weird laughing. I don't think I was scared. I don't remember being scared, anyway. Only curious. And maybe a little confused. The giggling was odd and out of place. Was there someone there that I didn't know about? Had my mom invited some guests without telling me?

My little brain just wanted to find an explanation. Like a sneaking cat, I followed my curiosity and the giggling into the living room.

I can still picture the way that our large brown sectional couch sat in the room. For whatever reason, my mother hadn't wanted the sectional placed too tightly into the corner. She wanted there to be a gap large enough for her to fit behind, instead of having the sectional budded up tight to the walls.

Maybe it was to make it easier to clean behind it.

Or possibly she had been afraid of me getting stuck between the sectional and the wall.

I don't recall.

After sneaking into the living room in search of the giggling, I paused for a moment to look around. My eyes instantly fell onto the right end of the sectional. I could see someone hiding in that gap and peeking out at me.

A tiny pale arm.

A pair of wide eyes.

"I found you!" I cried out, as if I had been in on the game the whole time.

A little girl, maybe six-years-old, lunged out and into my view. She had black hair that fell onto her shoulders and the largest green eyes I had ever seen. She was wearing a long, worn-out gray dress that nearly covered her ankles. And she was barefoot.

What stood out to me the most, and I can still clearly see it when I close my eyes, was the little girl's neck.

It was bent.

Not cocked to the side as if she were pondering a question.

But awkward, like how the arm is bent at the elbow.

At an angle a neck should never be.

Dorothy.

The girl never told me her name, but somehow, I knew it right away.

Dorothy.

I am still not sure why I wasn't scared. I should have been terrified. Years later, whenever I find myself thinking about that little girl, the hairs on my arms always stand on end. Maybe time and age bring clarity. But back then, the presence of Dorothy seemed as natural as the sun and the moon.

After jumping free of the sectional, Dorothy began laughing much louder than before. And, as she laughed, she began to spin around in place, as if she were a petite ballerina. Both her hair and the bottom of her dress puffed out as she twirled. And then, without warning, she rushed away.

And I chased her.

We ran circles throughout the bottom floor of the Red House, Dorothy always a few steps ahead of me. Her tiny legs were not very fast, but I don't think that I was actually trying to catch her.

The fun was in the chase.

It was a game.

She fled.

I pursued her.

And we both chuckled the entire time.

Dorothy and I were so loud that my mom ended up appearing at the top of the stairs, having been somewhere on the second floor. She shouted down, "What is with all the noise, Little Shane? Are the wild dogs chasing you again?"

I don't think that I answered her.

And my mom didn't really expect a reply, I don't believe, because she didn't wait long for one. A few seconds. Maybe. And then she disappeared again, back into whatever bedroom she was unpacking or organizing.

Just about the time when my short legs and small lungs began to burn, Dorothy made an unexpected shift and a sudden rush toward the steps.

***

Dorothy ran up the stairs.

No.

That is not right.

Dorothy didn't just run up the steps. She jumped and stomped her way towards the second floor, making as much commotion as she could along the way, laughing and laughing as she went, very much amusing herself.

How was she able to create so much commotion with such a tiny body?

I half-expected my mother to reappear and yell about the noise, but she never did.

When Dorothy finally reached the top of the stairs, she stopped and turned to me. I halted a couple of steps below and looked up at her. I had nearly forgotten about her bent neck, but as she looked down at me, that awkward angle was in full view.

It was still strange to see, but it no longer gave me the creeps.

There was a large grin spread across Dorothy's small, oval face, which was surprisingly still pale, like the skin of her arms. I had honestly expected her face to be red and flushed, like my sweaty mug, yet somehow she appeared as cool as a cucumber.

I was having fun playing with Dorothy and it seemed like the little girl was enjoying herself as well. With my mom still very busy unpacking and organizing our house, it was nice having someone to chase and laugh with. The loneliness and homesick feeling I had been experiencing had almost gone away. And, for a moment, I didn't think about my friend Taj.

I had a new friend.

Dorothy's smile was addictive, and I couldn't help but smile, too.

But then I remember my smile nearly slipping from my face, because as she stood proudly on top of the stairs, I got a closer look at Dorothy. What I had originally thought to be a faint shadow around her right eye turned out to be something else. It had faded quite a bit, but I could still make out the blue, black, and sickly green.

Several more spots of blue, black, and sickly green could be seen along her left arm, speckled mostly across her forearm and around her wrist.

A strange voice unexpectedly spoke from somewhere on the second floor, drawing my attention.

A man's voice.

It couldn't have been my dad.

As I said, he had been in the city.

The smile on Dorothy's face quickly vanished as the strange voice sprung up from behind her. Her eyes shot open wide, and I could tell that she was suddenly scared.

At first, the voice sounded muffled, discombobulated, but the angry tone was easily understood. It was coming from directly behind Dorothy. I moved my head this way and that way, trying to see around the little girl, to identify who was talking, but there didn't seem to be anyone standing there.

Dorothy turned away from me and peered into the empty space behind her.

"I'm sorry, daddy," she said to nothing.

The voice eventually became clear, and I could make out what the man was saying.

"I told you to stop playing on the stairs," said the angry man that I couldn't see. "You are too loud. You are being... too loud. You don't listen. You don't ever listen. If you don't want to do as you're told, I will have to make you. Now. Get off the stairs."

"Please, daddy," Dorothy pleaded. "Please. Don't."

I watched as an invisible force grabbed Dorothy by her black hair and pulled.

"Stop!" Dorothy continued to beg. "Hurts! I'm good! I'm good again, daddy!"

The invisible man didn't respond, but by the way Dorothy's hair was unexpectedly yanked harder, I believe that he attempted to drag her away from the top of the stairs.

Dorothy wasn't going willingly, however.

She fought and struggled against the angry man's grip, the whole time screaming to be let go.

I can't be sure if the man did let go or if Dorothy was able to break free, but the next thing that I remember was Dorothy stumbling backward, her hair no longer being pulled. When she stumbled, I realized that she had been standing too close to the top of the stairs.

But I made the realization too late.

"Nooooo," I screamed as I watched my new friend tumble down the steps. It all happened too fast, and I had been unable to grab a hold of her. I was helpless. As Dorothy fell, our eyes briefly met somehow, and I could feel her despair wash over me.

It was like being slammed with the coldest, heaviest wave.

And then I heard a loud, sickening snap when Dorothy reached the bottom.

I don't remember how long I stood there screaming, looking down at my new friend's lifeless body on the hardwood floor, before my mom appeared to curl her warm arms around me. My mom forced me to turn around and look into her loving eyes.

"What is wrong, Little Shane?" she asked.

But I couldn't answer.

I couldn't find the words.

I could only bury my face into her shoulder and cry, that sickening, snapping sound repeating over and over in my young brain.

After what must have been a few minutes, I found the courage to pull my head away from my mom and peer back to the bottom of the stairs.

Dorothy was gone.

***

That wasn't the only time that I played with Dorothy.

My mother and I only lived in the Red House with my father for two years. It took that long for my mom to figure out that, while she and I were living in a house in the country, my father's girlfriend was living in an apartment in the city.

Once that was discovered, it was easy to understand why my dad liked to spend long days away from home.

Whichever place, country or city, was actually home for him, anyway.

During those two years in the Red House, Dorothy returned every so often. Whenever she came around, I knew right away that she was there, because her giggling would give her away. We would always play the same game, running around, chasing and laughing. But the game inevitably ended the same way every time.

With the cracking of bone.

I tried a few times to keep Dorothy from running up the stairs, but it never worked. I tried grabbing her, but my arms only grabbed air. I tried yelling at her, but all she would do was laugh. It was pointless, and I eventually stopped trying. The cycle would repeat and there was nothing a little boy could do to stop it.

In the end, I just felt sorry for her, I guess.

After that first time, the shock and the terror of it, the sight of Dorothy dying affected me less and less, until I was numb to it completely.

I knew that she would be back.

I did eventually tell my mom about Dorothy, but I always left out the part about the invisible man and Dorothy falling down the stairs.

My mom always called Dorothy my imaginary friend, because no one else was ever able to see her. I knew the truth, though. Dorothy had not been imaginary. She had been something else entirely.

I can't say for sure why Dorothy showed herself to me back then.

Perhaps, she simply needed a new friend, too.

EVOLUTION INC.

THE SUBWAY TRAIN shot beneath the city like a shiny, elongated bullet, rubbing and vibrating against the thin metal rails. It sped, twisting and turning throughout New York's underbelly, the old decaying tunnels beneath the flourishing capital of the world.

Markus Salinger often wondered about the subway system. New York City seemed to be advancing at such a swift rate that everything was always newer and shinier every day, yet the subway tunnels looked as if they were about to crumble down around him. Why didn't they get an upgrade? With the sudden and unexpected popularity of monorails, why do subways even still exist? Maybe some old ideas simply refused to die.

The text of a science book, *Angels and Atoms*, filled a small computer screen, which extended from the arm of Markus' wheelchair. With his head tilted down toward the words, Markus read, trying to avoid any eye contact from other riders. However, a voice sang out from above, making him peek.

"Evol…"

The word Evol, in light blue, flowed through the flat television mounted above the nearby exit. The word also filled the many other screens throughout the subway car.

As the word faded, a woman with dark brown hair, curls falling to her shoulders, appeared on the screen wearing an all-blue jumpsuit. Her frame was petite and her buttermilk-colored skin was flawless, as if fake. She spoke: "The next step in humanity has arrived. Immortality is no longer myth or legend, but as real as your own mind."

Suddenly, the jumpsuit faded, and the woman was left naked. Her skin reminded Markus of smooth rubber. "On July 4th, join us here at Evol and let us take that next step together." Slowly, her skin faded, leaving a metallic android. "And skin will no longer hold us in. And death will no longer hold sway. It is time to shed our dying and live forever." The woman disappeared, leaving only the word Evol, and then that was also gone.

Markus lowered his eyes again but listened to the murmurs among some of the other passengers. He heard someone snicker and curse. He heard someone begin to pray to their God. Both responses were growing abundant these days.

Then Markus heard something that he had not experienced much of these days. Two seats down from Markus' personal chair, an elderly gentleman turned to his companion and whispered, "God bless them."

"Amen," the lady replied.

"I only wish that all of this had come sooner," the man said. "I would be first in line, by damned. Wouldn't that be nice, dear? Living together forever?" She simply nodded. "Today could be the day, you know. I hope so. Our time is almost up."

Markus' identification badge felt heavy in his shirt pocket. He would hurry, he thought to himself. Markus would hurry as if the Lord himself had kicked him in the ass. He would succeed too, not only for himself, but also for good people like the old gentleman and his lady.

The old man reminded Markus of someone. His grandfather.

***

The birds leaped and pecked at the falling breadcrumbs, while George Salinger giggled at the flapping feathers. "Aren't they beautiful, Markus?" George turned to his grandson and handed him a full piece of bread. "Break it up nice and small so that one bird won't hog the whole thing."

"Okay," Markus answered, fidgeting because the park bench was uncomfortable against his spine. With his short fingers, Markus began to break up the dry, stale piece of bread. "Okay," he repeated, wanting nothing but to impress his grandfather with his bread-breaking skills.

"All of the Lord's special animals were given wings," George said. "You hear me, Markus? Wings. That is how I know that humans are not God's chosen, because we were never given wings. Birds. Insects. Angels. Not mankind. Nope."

Markus continued to squirm as the ache rolled up and down the center of his back. Ignoring the pain, he threw out the crumbs as far as he could and watched as the little birds attacked.

"Birds. Insects. Angels."

"Not people," Markus added, his prepubescent voice cracking.

"What's wrong?" George asked, recognizing that Markus was fidgeting against the park bench.

"My back hurts," Markus replied.

"Again? You've been sitting here too long, is why," George told him. "Go play with the other children, over by the fountain. I can watch you from here. You do not need to keep an old man company. Go. Run. Be active."

Markus noticed the other kids, three of them, running and playing around the giant tree made of white stone. From several man-made pours built into the stone tree flowed streams of water. Dusk was near and the low sunlight reflected across the flowing water, giving it the illusion of liquid fire.

Markus sluggishly agreed to join the other kids, but when he jumped from the bench, his feet could not feel the ground. His entire body toppled over, causing Markus to cry out. He immediately reached for his legs, but without sensations, Markus could not at once find them.

***

Pushing a button, Markus scrolled to the next page in *Angels and Atoms* and came across a sentence that stood out. He finished reading it, went back, and then reread the sentence a second time. It was ironic that he would read this passage on this day.

The sentence went: *If science and faith refuse to find a common ground and work together, humankind will never progress any further.*

As Markus considered what he had read, the train's air brakes hissed, bringing the machine to a slow stop. Fresh passengers entered and tired commuters exited. Without completely raising his eyes, Markus noticed a woman and her young son come aboard. They sat directly across from Markus. He thought about nodding or smiling at them, but didn't.

Distant background noise suddenly became clear to Markus as CNN4 returned from a commercial break. The voice of a female broadcaster caught his attention.

"Evol," Susannah Prepon began, before pausing to shuffle her notecards. "The self-proclaimed 'makers of miracles' hope to accomplish their grandest miracle to date. A miracle worthy of the Almighty himself. One that they simply call Angel.

"They will do this today. July 4th. A day known in history as the celebration of independence and freedom. Is there symbolism in using this day? One can only speculate."

Another train stop came and went, doors opened and closed, but Markus kept his attention on the television.

"The mystery of the human brain has been solved, or so Evol claims," the woman continued. "And according to Evol, this long-awaited triumph comes with an endless array of possibilities. An end to disease. An end to hunger. Maybe even an end to death. But how?

"And what exactly is Angel? Apparently, according to an Evol spokesperson, the human mind works like an advanced computer, only specific to each and every person. But a computer nonetheless. Like the data on your computer, everything in it that makes it unique can be transferred to another system. And this idea is the foundation for Angel.

"The Evol spokesperson refused to give any more details. But through commercials that have been running for several weeks, the idea is pretty obvious. Humans could become robots.

"There is one man, though, who refuses to stand by and let this happen."

A picture of Senator Long appeared in the corner, his dark eyes sitting behind thick-rimmed glasses.

"Senator Arthur Long," the woman continued, "is angry. 'They are going to take away our flesh and replace it with metal. They want us all to be robots,' Long has been quoted as saying.

"Senator Long is an active leader of a growing movement known as Skin Against Metal, or S.A.M, who are, at the moment, continuing their stern protests outside of Evol Headquarters in New York. Senator Long, a war veteran, has adamantly spoken out against Evol and the use of cybernetics.

"Senator Long promises that the protests will remain peaceful, but some worry that the growing tension, which has been building steadily over that past year or so, will erupt very soon.

"Could the members of S.A.M. and the supporters of Evol ever find common ground, or will this turn into a bitter battle for years to come? We will have to wait and see." With these final words, a male newscaster appeared on the screen and began to report on the peace treaty between China and North Korea, which did not interest Markus.

Wait and see.

No more waiting. Today the world will see, Markus was thinking, when suddenly he recognized a young man that was sitting several feet from him.

Markus knew the face.

But how?

When the young man returned Markus' creepy stare, it came back to him.

Johnny.

His name was Johnny.

And Johnny's right eye was a portion of a second slower than the other, because it was robotic. Markus recalled that Johnny's real eye had been torn out by a dog as a toddler.

Evol.

That was how Markus recognized Johnny. But did Johnny recognize Markus in return? Probably not. Markus had handled the case from a distance, never meeting the young man face-to-face.

Why did Johnny continue to stare then, even after Markus had stopped? Markus already knew the answer. The young man, like many others, was staring at the cripple, a broken man in a world where nothing seemed to remain broken for too long. If a toddler was made whole after an angry dog had taken his eye, why couldn't Markus be made whole too?

***

"What about robotics?" George Salinger asked, trying to keep his voice from shaking as he spoke to Dr. Peterson. "I hear there are lots of improvements in the field. Reconstruction. Rebuilding. Cybernetics. Replacing bones and even organs."

Dr. Peterson replied, "True, cybernetics is rapidly growing, but I do not believe that would be able to help your grandson, Mr. Salinger."

"Can't they rebuild or replace whatever is broken? If they can build an entire working arm for that Marine over in the desert, can't they rebuild or fix my grandchild?"

Markus sat next to his grandfather, taking in the conversation with only half attention. It was difficult for him to focus when he was so dreadfully uncomfortable. He tried to adjust his spine by fidgeting, but the warm pain remained.

"His brain is faulty, Mr. Salinger," the doctor answered. "That is the major problem here. The brain is having problems sending and receiving signals with the body. And the brain will eventually lose signal completely with certain parts of the body, like the legs, for example. There is just no way for us to build or engineer parts of the brain. It is too complex for any kind of machinery to replicate. It can't be done right now; it may never be possible."

George Salinger looked defeated. "Is there anything that we can do for him?"

"The signals have begun to slowly deteriorate," Dr. Peterson said. "But it will take time for them to completely shut down. The lack of sensation and movement ability that Markus is experiencing right now is temporary but will eventually become permanent."

"Okay."

Dr. Peterson continued. "I know of a medication that might work at slowing down the deterioration. That would be our best option right now. His body and his brain are having problems with their communication, Mr. Salinger, and this med will work as an intermediary, like a marriage counselor, or a preacher talking to God for his congregation."

"What about the pain?"

"Markus seems to be feeling mild discomfort right now," Dr. Peterson began, "but the pain will slowly intensify over the years. The medication will not help with that pain. We should start Markus on a pain management regimen as soon as possible. We don't want to rely completely on drugs. We are going to use other forms of pain management, as well."

"Thank you, Dr. Peterson."

"Don't give up hope," Dr. Peterson said. "Evol is still considered to be a young pup and we are still growing, and miracles happen here every day."

***

The lobby of Evol Headquarters was nearly empty, with only one receptionist and two guards watching the front entrance of glass. Though empty, the main lobby was far from quiet. The doors were not soundproof, and the roar of the outside protesters traveled easily through the wide-open room. Markus felt the vibrations as he steered his chair into the elevator.

Markus knew that the rest of the building would be nearly as empty. Any employees not assigned to Angel had been told to remain at home. The possibility of an aggravated outburst by the protesters made it necessary that only the bare essential staff were here, and most were waiting for Markus on the 38th floor.

Markus had come into the building by way of the subway entrance, positioned on the side, away from the view of the protesters. He had to use it because the front doors were to remain locked. The subway entrance was rarely used, and Markus was not entirely sure why it even existed. It required an I.D. card swipe, retina scan, and voice recognition to activate. With all the precautions, Markus could not help but feel a sense of impending doom, and it made him a little nervous.

With the tiny joystick on the armrest, Markus turned his chair 180 degrees to face the elevator's panel. "Doors close," he muttered, and once they had slid shut, he reached into the shirt's front pocket for his I.D. card. Suddenly, his left arm began to tremble uncontrollably. His spine and left forearm filled with liquid fire. A harsh breath escaped him while the pain continued to flow and burn him on the inside.

The tremble in his arm became a familiar convulsion. Using his right arm, Markus clutched the other and forced it on to the armrest. Quickly, yet carefully, he managed to lock two straps across his left arm, keeping it secure.

Markus had taken his meds already. It was too soon to take them again. Opening a compartment in the top of the right armrest, Markus plucked out a vial tipped with a needle. Looking at his still-shaking arm, Markus knew that he would never hit a vein. He took several seconds to consider the options, and the overwhelming pain chose for him. Swiftly, he stabbed the needle into the side of his neck and injected it. The drug was cold as it spread out and doused the fire in seconds.

However, the shaking continued.

Swiping the I.D. card, mumbling, "38th floor," Markus got the elevator to move, and he began to ascend the tower.

As Markus rolled from the elevator and into his lab, he noticed there were two groups of people waiting for him: the executive suits, and the lab assistants. The sum of them barely made a dozen. Millions of lives might rest upon this test, Markus knew, but only a handful of people would actually witness it. He wondered if this was how it felt the day that they tested the first atomic bomb, quiet suits and assistants willing to change the world.

"Big day, Markus," CEO Stockholm said, his hair and his suit black.

Markus ignored the words as he glided past the tie-wearing men and women. He headed directly toward the row of windows behind his desk. Through the tall windows, Markus looked out across a sea of people that hated him and hated what he was trying to do. He could not help but hate them back.

The crowd had to be reaching close to a thousand or more. They did not block the streets, but instead filled Fruition Garden, a strip of land across from Evol Headquarters. Evol had bought the plot and torn down the abandoned hospital that had once sat there. Over several months, Evol covered the seemingly useless piece of Earth with soil and flowers and trees and sculptures of animals and people.

At the center of this beautiful garden was a giant marble fountain in the shape of the Tree of Life, streams of water flowing out from within the bark. Markus loved to sit and stare at the garden. He was reminded of childhood times with his grandfather. Now the garden may be forever tainted.

Forming a human barrier between the protesters and Evol Headquarters were the city police officers. And they were dressed in full riot gear. A precaution, Markus assumed. But the police presence at Kent State University in 1970 might have started as a simple precaution, as well.

Markus glared at the massive crowd. He was looking for a podium or a stage, any place from which Senator Long would speak.

And Senator Long *would* speak.

Markus knew that.

Giving up the search, Markus reached with his steady hand and slid the window open. A roar flooded into the once sound-proofed room.

"I want to hear them," Markus stated. "I want to hear them all."

Markus turned and once again wheeled past the suits, this time going to a large computer terminal. His assistants remained motionless, simply watching. Everything was already prepared, waiting for Markus to finish. They were merely present in case something went wrong.

"Your arm, Mr. Salinger," assistant Ross pointed out.

Markus shook his head.

"Salinger. Password: Prometheus," Markus spoke, bringing the computer screen to life. "Open Markus Salinger Mental Scan." A virtual file appeared and then opened, spilling out images. At the top left corner was Markus, his full body profile slowly spinning. Next to his profile was a digital brain, spotted by blues and reds.

Across the bottom, waves flowed from left to right. All of this was Markus, not the skin but the presence. Every neuron and cell and connection and misfire that was Markus Salinger had been mapped, scanned, and downloaded into this computer, faulty wiring not included.

Or so he hoped.

Before Markus could continue, a voice boomed from outside. "They want us to shed our skin," Senator Long began, his powerful voice filling large speakers. "They want us to give up the very gift that God has given us. Our flesh. They say that they can make us live a longer life, possibly forever. No more sickness or dying. What about our souls? They say that we are nothing but firing neurons. But are our souls nothing but neurons? No. Our souls are more. Our souls are our one true link to the Lord above. And they are treating it as just another computer glitch. Who do they think they are? God? No. They are not God."

"No!" over a thousand mouths replied.

Markus had heard enough.

"Activate Angle One Program," he proclaimed.

***

"Soldier refuses cybernetic legs," a voice said from the television, causing Markus to halt his pen tip and look up from his desk. As usual, CNN4 was on the television, mainly for background noise. Markus knew the voice to be Alan Cummings. "Colonel Arthur Long, a soldier with the United States Army, and his unit were ambushed by a group of hostiles during a daily patrol yesterday. After nearly an hour of exchanging bullets, Colonel Long managed to fix a broken radio and call for reinforcements. But while reinforcements were en route, an explosion hit Colonel Long, damaging both of his legs, to the point that they had to be removed.

"Since the colonel was a decorated soldier wounded in the line of duty, the government was willing to pay the bill for a pair of cybernetic limbs. The legs would work and feel like his own legs, along with the sensation of touch and pain. But Colonel Long turned the offer down."

Markus' hand tensed and his grip tightened around the blue pen.

"When asked why, Colonel Long had this to say…"

Colonel Long appeared on the screen, "It is God's will that I lost my legs. I don't feel that it is my right to try to replace them with metal ones, even if that means that I have to spend the rest of my life in a chair. That is God's will."

God's will? Markus grew angry. He looked around his tiny office, remembering why he was at Evol and all that he wished to accomplish. The hard work. Two college degrees. The debt. The nerve of that man. How could anyone turn down the chance to walk, the chance to run alongside everyone else? Markus pointlessly hurled the pen at the television screen and watched it harmlessly bounce off.

***

Markus returned to consciousness and was immediately confused. He didn't remember falling asleep. He was lying on something hard, possibly metal, and it was giving him sensations in his spine, but for the first time in many years, it wasn't discomfort. It wasn't… pain. It was some other kind of sensation. He couldn't place the feeling. It was different.

Another set of sensations called for Markus' attention, not because they were different, but because they should not exist at all. He could feel his legs, both of them.

Opening his eyes, Markus was bombarded by light, which was overwhelming for a second, but quickly focused. Rising to sit, Markus turned to let his feet fall and touch the floor. The floor held a chill, the most wonderful chill that he had ever felt.

Markus was in his own lab; he knew that much. At once, Markus saw himself, still in the wheelchair, and staring back. There were others in the room as well, also staring. For a moment, he was startled, but then he realized what must have been taking place.

Markus was now Angel.

Angel saw that he was naked except for a pair of white boxer-briefs. He admired himself. He was perfect. Every inch of his new skin was flawless. He was muscular, like the statue of David. This was him now, he knew. And he loved the idea.

The roar continued to pulse throughout the room, and Angel, after removing a few wires that were stuck to his shaved skull, went to the open window to peer down upon them. He ignored the CEO, who tried to speak to him. Angel was only interested in the protesters. He could see them clearly, every head, every hair, each and every smirk, as if they were inches away.

Angel could also hear them individually, instead of in an overwhelming bundle. He could especially hear Senator Long, who continued to preach. Angel isolated the voice. He might be able to follow it.

Without warning, Angel broke out the window's screen and leaped through. He allowed the Earth to pull him, but only briefly. The fall was incredible. Angel felt the rushing air brush every inch of his skin. Pleasure signals sped throughout his body. But the exhilaration of the plunge was short-lived. Angel's wings opened. He felt the feathers grab the air.

The sky was a clear blue.

A nice day for a flight.

Following the voice of Senator Long, Angel flew toward a short podium sitting beside the Tree of Life. Angel could clearly see Long, in his permanent sitting position, gripping the microphone as if he were speaking to the entire world. In some way, he might be.

One-by-one, people in the crowd began to notice Angel. Their alerted heads shifted in a massive wave.

"They have done it!" Senator Long screamed into the microphone. "They have dethroned God! They have damned us all!"

Swiftly, the crowd imploded. The police had no choice but to respond. Angel was stunned at how immediately the violence came. Why couldn't they understand? Didn't they see the perfection?

But then something went wrong. Both of his legs began to twitch and then shake before going completely numb. "No," Angel grunted. His brain had been scanned, but the underlying problem, the one that Markus had been convinced had been left behind with the flesh, still existed. It had been more deeply rooted than Markus had realized.

Angel cursed and damned his creator.

His right wing went limp, sending him spiraling toward the crowd. He fought, left wing flapping crazily, but he landed nonetheless.

The crowd of suits turned to Markus to shake their heads. They had watched the rise and the fall from their tower.

"Angel One… failure," Markus told the computer. The screen was already filling up with data being thrown back to them from the fallen Angel. What had been the mistake? Markus would know soon enough and then he could fix it, then he could move on to Angel Two.

It took God six steps to make the world, but maybe it would only take Markus two steps to change it.

BLACK ICE

I HAD BEEN on the road for over five hours before I finally decided to pull over to take a piss. I was making good time, but I couldn't wait any longer. My bladder was full of Monster, along with other assorted caffeinated beverages, and the bastard was screaming at me to release the pressure. At that point in my travels, I was in between major highways, and I wasn't sure when I would come across another gas station, or bathroom of any kind.

No big deal, I figured.

Urinating at the side of the road would work. Nature would have to be my bathroom. Luckily, it was the middle of the night and traffic had been nonexistent for some time.

I would have hated for a cop to come by and catch me dangling in the wind.

I quickly swung my car into the first dirt pull-off I came across and slammed it into park. I left the motor running, as I opened the door and jumped from the vehicle. There wasn't much light in the middle of nowhere and I would need my car's headlights to see. Ain't nothing more dangerous than pissing in the dark. You never know what you might hit when you can't see shit.

You might even hit yourself by accident. And I wasn't trying to smell like piss the rest of the way.

I guess I could've changed into one of the other pairs of my jeans I had stuffed into the back of my car, if need be, but why take unnecessary risks?

A blast of icy air struck me as I got out of the car and immediately made my bladder scream even louder. No. It hadn't been screaming at that point. The bastard had been howling, like a cold dog howling at the moon. Jogging to the other side of my car, I swiftly unzipped my jeans and ignored the full-body shiver that hit me when I exposed myself to the cold night. The mixture of warm piss and cold air caused me to feel contradicting sensations in my nether regions. I closed my eyes and I let out a loud sigh of relief as my bladder began to empty.

Once I was finished and tucked away, I didn't at once rush back to the warmth of my car. The chill wasn't bothering me as much and I decided to take a moment to enjoy the peaceful quiet of the night.

I peered down from the top of a steep embankment and out over a dark valley. Filling the valley was a thick forest that appeared to stretch on for a few miles. From where I stood, I couldn't see any lights, not from houses or businesses or other possible forms of civilization. I was in no man's land. Or at least I would have been until I eventually met up with State Route 33, a four-lane highway that would take me the rest of the way. There also didn't seem to be a whole lot of movement or normal sounds coming from the trees, either, except for a low serenade from a far-off owl.

Maybe, since an inch or two of snow covered everything, the forest animals had decided to chill out for the night. All except for that single owl who just kept singing on and on.

It had been snowing most of the day and into the night, until finally stopping about a half-hour before. Thankfully, it had been the light, fluffy stuff that doesn't stick well to the roads. If it had been that heavy, slushy shit, then it would have slowed me down and pissed me off.

I always hated snow, but for some reason I have always lived in places that get a shit ton of it every winter.

With everything around me being still and tranquil, it helped to temporarily calm my constantly racing mind, which had been a welcome change. I had done nothing but hurry, hurry, hurry for the prior few days and it was nice to just stop for a minute to breathe.

My marriage had fallen apart, to put it mildly. To put it honestly, my marriage had exploded like the fucking time bomb it had always been. Four years of building pressure, like piss in a bladder, until it finally went… *boom*. I let her have whatever she wanted, because I just didn't care. There hadn't been much to fight over, anyway. We didn't own a house or have kids, thank God. We had a tiny, ugly dog, but that had always been her baby. Not mine. I hated that dog. In the end, I managed to walk away from the devastation with what I could fit in my car.

And having your entire life fit into a blue Chevy Impala can put things into perspective, let me tell you.

When I was 18, like most naïve assholes, I couldn't have run away from home fast enough. I had dreams to chase, mistakes to make, and a crazy bitch to marry. But when the dust settled on my marriage, that was where I was headed back to. Home. My real home. And I couldn't get back to my parents and the town I grew up in fast enough.

As I continued to peer into the distance, I could see the black outline of the Appalachian Mountains standing tall on the horizon, barely visible against the night sky. Black on black has a way of blending together. With the mountains in my sights, I knew that my destination was only a few more hours away.

A pair of headlights suddenly pulled me from my thoughts, two bright orbs coming down the stretch of road I was standing beside. They were headed in the direction I had been coming from. Damn. The vehicle's high beams momentarily blinded me, but I threw both of my hands up real quick. I was able to partially block out the bright light until it shifted away from my eyes and I could see again. When the headlights from my own car fell across this new arrival, I could tell that it was a car smaller than my Chevy.

A compact.

Possibly foreign.

Dark blue.

My Impala's headlights also fell on something else, a massive patch of ice on the road. The spot of ice was several yards long and wide enough to take up an entire lane of the road, while still having enough width to spill over into the other lane, as well. Normally, black ice didn't scare me. It wasn't the evil villain some people made it out to be. Yet, by how clearly the surface reflected the moon, which had finally found a space between clouds from which to peek out, I could tell that the ice was thick and solid.

There was nothing I could have done but hope that the approaching compact car had good tires and a calm driver. Maybe the driver would notice the ice and take the other lane to avoid it. That was what I would have done. There hadn't been any oncoming traffic, making that the smart choice.

But the driver never saw the black ice.

Instead, the compact car took it dead center.

From start to finish, everything that happened next only took a few seconds.

The compact car began to slide as soon as it hit the ice. Its back end started to spin out. Rather than make a slight adjustment in the steering, I helplessly watched the driver panic. As the driver slammed on the brakes and pulled hard on the wheel, squealing tires replaced the once tranquil silence.

The little car spun and spun fast.

It spun out onto the other lane and cleared the ice. At that point, the driver should have hit the brakes, but the driver was still panicked. I could hear the car's engine rev as the driver stomped hard on the gas. The wheels chose then to gain traction, which sent the car barreling across the road and over the edge of the embankment.

At the sight of the car spilling over the edge, I instantly dashed toward the other side of the pull off. Standing and looking down off the ledge, I could see the glow of two headlights rushing down the steep drop. Somehow, the car managed to almost make it down the entire decline without hitting one of the trees growing from the side of the hill.

I don't want to call it luck that the car didn't hit a tree earlier in the fall, because it might have been better off striking one of the trees growing closer to the top. By the time it hit one near to the ground, gravity had been pulling hard on that car. Not even the snow did much to slow it down once gravity had its hands on it.

I can't say exactly how fast the car was going when it finally hit. But when it did hit that tree, the sound of the impact, the twisting of metal and the breaking of glass, shattered both the night and my mind into a million fragments. I don't want to be a drama queen, but it all sank into me deeply, all the way to my core. Whenever I try to sleep at night, I can still hear the destruction of that car getting wrapped around that tree.

My phone!

That was my first clear thought. I needed to call for help. If the driver was still alive, I needed to get someone there to help them. If the driver wasn't... someone still needed to be there to deal with it.

After realizing that I had left my cell in the Chevy, I turned to run back and get it, but something stopped me from moving.

A woman screaming.

"Help me! Please! Somebody, please help me!"

The screams were obviously coming from down the embankment, from the wrecked car.

I tried to find a strong voice and yell back. I couldn't get as loud as I wanted to, but I did my best, anyway. "It's gonna be okay! Just hang tight! I am going to call for help!"

The woman's voice became shrill and terror-stricken.

"Oh my god! Oh my god! Help me!"

Before I realized what I was doing, I was making my way down the hill. The moon had retreated back behind the dense clouds, throwing a thick shadow over everything. As I rushed through the dense night, I aimed myself away from the lights of my Impala and toward the headlights of the wreckage. I clearly remember having images of burning cars and burning people flashing through my head. I didn't see any flames, but there might be smoke. It would've been difficult to see dark smoke when everything else was just as dark.

I had to act. I had to do something. I had to be sure that woman was not going to fucking burn to death while I sat on the phone with 911 waiting for help to eventually show up. If that happened, I would have never forgiven myself.

The Nikes that I had been wearing were a far cry from hiking boots. They were not meant for descending a steep, slick hill. Several times the snow tried to bring me down, take both of my feet from under me, but each time I somehow managed to grab onto a nearby tree trunk or bush and stay upright.

I was moving as fast as I could, but I didn't know if it was fast enough to matter.

The woman had grown silent after the last nearly hysterical howl. I began to fear what I might find.

Keeping the headlights in front of me, I was able to find the wreckage in the blackness of night. And it was as bad as I had thought. The entire front of the compact car had been caved in, crushed into the shape of a large, jagged horseshoe. I don't understand how the headlights were still shining. There was a little bit of smoke rising from the car, but it wasn't black smoke from active burning. It was light and faint, probably from the car's small engine being obliterated. And I didn't smell any flames, either.

Yet, fire suddenly became the least of my concerns. The way the car had brutally imploded against that damned tree immediately painted a different picture in my mind. At least, my rushing thoughts were no longer of burning women. But images of death still filled my brain.

The driver had been alive and screaming for me, but that didn't mean she was still breathing. Part of me didn't want to go around to the driver's side of the car, but I needed to be sure.

"Ma'am!" I called out, as I rushed around the back of the vehicle.

No answer.

"Are you okay, ma'am?"

Silence.

When I made it to the other side of the car, I saw that the driver's window had been shattered, completely destroyed. I briefly stopped. The inside of the car was dark and hard to see into, just like everything else that fucked up night. As I fought against my rapid breathing, I reluctantly leaned in closer so that I could get a better look through the non-existent window.

Someone was sitting in the driver's seat.

"Ma'am?" I said. "Are you okay, ma'am?"

It was a petite young woman. Light brown hair pulled in a tight ponytail. Mid-20s perhaps.

But she never moved or replied. She couldn't. She just stared at me. Her neck twisted at an awkward angle. Wide-eyed. Forever afraid of what was about to happen to her. She hadn't been wearing her seatbelt, and the airbag malfunctioned. When her face hit the steering wheel, the force nearly spun her head clean around.

Dead on impact.

Before the accident, the young woman might have been kind of pretty... in a simple kind of way.

That was when I smelled the cloud of alcohol escaping through the car window. I didn't search to find the source. I already knew what it was.

I then remember my heart sinking as a realization hit me. If she had been dead on impact, then who the hell had been screaming at me? A passenger? I looked around the inside of the car, or what was left of it, but I didn't see anyone else. The passenger side was empty, and the door was still closed. The backseat was empty, too.

The hair on the back of my neck stood up when I then heard the same woman's voice.

"Help!"

It came from behind me, from somewhere in the trees.

"Somebody help me! Who are you!? Get away from me! Don't touch me! Help!"

I could feel the fear in her voice. I could feel it as if it were my own.

"Get away from me!"

Someone else had been in the car. That had been my immediate assumption.

With the trees creating a million little echoes, it was hard to pinpoint from exactly which direction the voice was coming. When I thought that I knew the general area I needed to go toward, I took off running. For several more seconds, the woman continued to cry for help, but ultimately the words died and all that remained were frightened screams.

I yelled back once. I wanted her to know that I was coming.

"Don't be scared! I'm here!"

I used her voice to guide me, because, other than that, I was running blind. But I found her. Somehow. She must have heard me, because when I got there, she at once turned her head my way. She was a petite woman. Somewhere in her mid-20s. Light brown hair pulled in a tight ponytail. Kind of pretty, in a simple kind of way. Her eyes wide with fear.

I knew that face. I had seen it only moments before. It was the driver. But how? Twins? No. I can't explain it, but I knew that I was looking into the face of the same, dead woman.

She was on her butt in the snow with her back against a tree trunk. The way she was pressed up against the base of the tree, it was like she was fending off a wild animal. But I didn't see any wolves or bears or coyotes.

As I looked down on her, the words rose into my throat before I realized I was speaking. "I'm here to help.

Don't be scared." But I felt the words to be hollow. There was no help for her. And she may have been scared. But so was I. And there was no changing it.

"Who are they?" she asked me. "Why are they after me?"

"Who is after you?" I replied. I searched the area again, but I couldn't see anyone else but the two of us. "I don't know what you mean."

She then raised her arm and pointed to a spot a couple of feet from where she sat.

"Them. Don't you see them?"

At first, I didn't. I couldn't.

But when I opened my mouth to assure her that no one was there, the moon peeked from the clouds again, casting beams of light down on us. The light revealed something that I had not noticed a second before. Two figures standing in the exact spot the woman was pointing. They were human-like in form. Short. Closer to the height of a child than an adult. And they were pure black from head to toe. No faces or features of any kind.

Just darkness as deep as I imagine a black hole to be.

A bottomless void.

But they were also smooth looking, polished. I could only see them with help from the moon, because the moonlight reflected across the two figures in the same way it had the patch of black ice.

There had been a stillness about them, or at least there was until the moon showed them to me. When it was obvious that I could now see them too, the two black figures rushed at the woman. It was so easy for them to grab her, to snatch her by her legs. There was nothing that she or I could do to stop it.

I don't know why they waited that long to take her. Maybe they had been playing with her until I showed up. I'm not sure. I will never be sure.

Once the two figures had a hold of her legs, they began to drag her away. She screamed and desperately tried to grab ahold of the tree trunk, but there was no chance of her holding on. They drug her off through the snow and into the woods.

I can still picture her face as they drug her away. The terror. The helplessness. It's seared into my brain. She had looked to me for help, but I couldn't do anything. I had been useless. Or could I have actually helped her, somehow? Could I have kept those… things… from grabbing her? No. There was nothing I could have done.

For a second after the woman was pulled off, I was frozen by my fear. I did my best to shake it off and chase after them, but they were already out of sight. Even though I had watched her get dragged off through the snow, there was no physical path of any kind for me to follow, no trail of disturbed snow. It was fucking weird. So instead, I tried to follow the only thing that I had, the woman's horrific screaming. But even that became further and further away, until finally fading away completely, swallowed by the night.

I don't know why I started yelling. I didn't know what else to do.

"Can you hear me! Keep screaming so I can find you!"

I'm not sure how long I stood there, cold and shaking. But I continued to listen for her. For any signs of her. But there was nothing. I don't know where the two figures took her, but they were long gone.

At some point, I was able to gather my thoughts and navigate my way back to the wreckage by following the glow of the headlights. From there, I made my way back to my own car, again by following the glow of headlights. Getting back up the embankment was much slower and way more difficult than going down it.

But I managed.

I found my cell in my Chevy, where I knew it had been plugged in and charging. Before I dialed 911, I took a couple of minutes to mentally rehearse what I was going to say. I couldn't completely lie, but I wasn't going to tell them everything. I would have sounded fucking crazy. When the emergency operator answered my call, I told him that a car had wrecked on black ice and hit a tree. I had gone down the embankment to try to help. My tracks in the snow would have told them that, whether I wanted to or not. But when I got to the crash, the driver was already dead. Killed on impact. I went back to my car, got my cell phone, and called them.

End of story.

At least as far as they knew.

But I can't help but wonder what those creatures were and whether or not they would come for me when it was my time.

I DREAMED OF MONSTERS

I HAD BEEN daydreaming, existing somewhere between awake and asleep, a realm I had become quite familiar with over the past few weeks. When a female voice called my name, "Darryl Rashad," I became startled and nearly jerked out of my seat. Luckily, I was the last appointment of the day and there wasn't anyone else in the waiting room to see my embarrassment.

Aside from Dr. Pemberton, anyway.

I rose from my chair without a word and slowly followed the psychologist into her office, my head down as if I was being marched to the guillotine. In a way, I felt like I had been beheaded a long time ago, yet, for some reason, my body continued moving forward.

"Have a seat," Dr. Pemberton instructed, pointing to a large comfortable looking blue chair. It was a similar type of chair that was in my Grammy's house. It had a high back and was nearly long enough for two people. The cushions were very thick and very soft.

Yep.

Exactly like the one my Grammy Eustace had.

I remembered being ten years old and curling up in my Grammy's living room chair. I loved that chair. I had some of the best naps in it. I could fall asleep for hours and never move. I wish that I could sleep like that again, like a child without a care in the world. As does our innocence, that type of sleep leaves us whenever we become adults.

"Darryl?"

The psychologist's voice broke through from far off. She sat only several feet away, but she could easily have been on the moon. Damn. I had been drifting off for what must have been the hundredth time that day.

"I'm sorry," I replied. "I keep spacing out."

"You still look very tired," Dr. Pemberton said. "Have you been sleeping any better? The sleep aids haven't been working?"

"They help me fall asleep," I replied. "But… when I need to wake up… when the dream happens… I get stuck sometimes. The dream just repeats over and over, and I can't get out. So, I stopped taking them. I'd rather not sleep at all than get stuck in that nightmare loop."

Dr. Pemberton nodded.

"I understand," she said. "The dream hasn't gotten any better?"

"No!" I spat. "The dream hasn't gotten any better or any worse! It is still the same exact fucking dream every time, like I told you!" My voice then quieted. "I am sorry. I am… I am sorry. I shouldn't have yelled. I just feel like I am losing my mind. My eyes hurt and feel like sandpaper. I barely have the energy to breathe or chew food. I feel like I am underwater all the time. And everything else in the world… doesn't feel real. It all seems fake, like an illusion that I am no longer a part of. I don't know how much longer I can do this. I… need… to… sleep."

"Something else happened," Dr. Pemberton said. "Hasn't it?"

"My girlfriend…" I began, but then paused.

"How is your girlfriend?" she asked. "Trista? Right?"

"Right," I replied. "She was staying over at my apartment a couple of nights ago. I was having that dream again and I must have been thrashing around and I… I must have hit her."

"Is she okay?" Dr. Pemberton asked.

"A black eye," I explained.

"You do know that it wasn't your fault?"

"Yes," I replied. "She understands that I didn't mean to do it, either. But I am not *okay* with it. Not at all. I want the nightmare to stop. It needs to stop or… I don't know. It just needs to stop. Maybe I should commit myself. I don't know what else to do. Why is this happening to me?"

"As I said before," she explained in her unnervingly calm voice, "night terrors are not all that uncommon. Trust me, you are not going crazy. And night terrors are very treatable. We will fix this, Darryl. I promise. And all this will feel like a bad dream, pun intended. I hope that makes you feel a little better, at least."

"I wish it did," I replied.

"Me too," Dr. Pemberton nodded. "Okay. Now. Let's talk about the dream again. I want you to take me through it. From start to finish. What happens?"

"We already did this," I exhaled. I didn't want to conjure up the nightmare. I wanted to pretend that it didn't exist, at least for a little while. I wanted to push it from my mind so that I had a little bit of temporary peace. I knew that the horror would be waiting for me whenever I tried to sleep that night. If I even tried to sleep. I would have to worry about that whenever the time came.

Burn that bridge when I get there, so to speak.

"I believe that there is an underlying cause that we need to figure out," Dr. Pemberton said. "Recurring dreams are rarely random. They usually mean something to the person having them. Your brain is trying to give you information, but it is jumbled or lost in translation, making it come across as a puzzle, a terrifying one, in your case. If we figure out the puzzle, then maybe we can get the dream to stop."

"You really think so?"

"I do."

"It is always the same dream," I began, as I closed my tired, aching eyes. "I think that I am around eight years old and I am asleep in my bed. I wake up when I hear someone moving around in my room. At first, I thought that it was my mom or my dad. But then I smell it. Something stinks. Like something dead."

"Last time you said that it smelled like roadkill?"

"That's right," I replied. "My mom or dad don't smell that way, so I open my eyes and I see the monster standing over my bed, looking down at me."

"What does the monster look like?"

"In the dream," I continued, "it is tall and thin. It has really long arms and legs. It's naked, but I can't make out any private parts. Its skin is like a sickly brownish grey. It has random patches of hair on its head. Its face doesn't seem straight, if that makes sense. Everything is... crooked. And it is holding a large, pale sack, an old-timey feed sack."

"Sounds pretty scary."

"Yeah," I said. "When I see the monster, I try to scream, but it stuffs something in my mouth. Its hands are like leather. Long fingers. Long sharp nails. I want to fight, but I am not strong enough. The monster ties my hands and feet and then grabs me from my bed. It stuffs me into its sack and then carries me off."

"Then what?"

"The monster always takes me to the same place," I replied. "The vegetable cellar behind the house that my dad built into the side of the hill."

"What happens after you are in the cellar?"

I shuddered.

"The monster," I continued, "it dumps me from the sack onto the floor. For nearly a minute, it just stares at me, like it's hungry and I am a juicy steak. I want to run away, but my hands and feet are still tied. Also, the monster blocks the cellar door."

I paused.

"And then what happens?"

"I..." I began, but immediately stopped. I have a hard time finding the words, but eventually mumble, "The monster... eats me."

"It eats you? How so?"

"It doesn't only bite into me," I said, "like you see in movies. It also uses its sharp claws and tears my skin away piece by piece. It just rips me apart and eats the chunks. I can hear it chewing me. It's wet and sloppy. I usually wake up when it breaks my ribs and tears out my beating heart."

A moment passed in silence before Dr. Pemberton decided to speak.

"In the dream, where are you?"

"At home," I replied. "I mean, the house I grew up in."

"It's always the same house?" she asked. "You are always the same age?"

I nodded.

"I lived there with my mom and dad until I was about nine," I responded.

"How are your memories of living there?" Dr. Pemberton asked.

"I don't have a lot of them," I said. "I can't even tell you what town we lived in."

"That is understandable," Dr. Pemberton replied. "Trauma at an early age can affect memory."

"I do remember bits and pieces," I said. "I can still picture my bedroom. I like basketball and I remember I had some basketball posters on my wall. I'm not sure what teams or what players, though. I can't really remember much about how the house looked. But I remember there were a lot of trees around. No other houses. It wasn't in town, or anything. It was in the country. In the woods. I don't remember if I had any friends or what school was like. I don't remember any of that kind of stuff. I don't really remember much at all."

"You remember the cellar out behind the house, though?"

"Vaguely," I said. "I think I watched my dad dig into the hill when he was building it. I'm not sure. My mom used it to store our potatoes. I think. And she canned vegetables and kept them there, too. I don't remember it being very big. In the dream, it feels really small. I mainly remember the smell. The inside smelled like stale dirt."

"Why did you move away from the house?" Dr. Pemberton asked.

"You already know the answer!" I blurted.

I was beginning to get aggravated because she kept asking me questions that I had already answered. I wanted new questions. New answers. New solutions. I didn't understand how going in circles was going to help me.

"I want to hear you say it again," Dr. Pemberton said.

"I went to live with my Grammy Eustace," I replied.

"Why?"

"Both my parents died," I said.

"How did they die?"

"What the fuck are we doing?" I cursed again, but didn't apologize that time. Instead, I pretended like it never happened. "They are both dead. Doesn't matter how or why."

"I think it is obviously connected," Dr. Pemberton said. "But I don't think that the memories of your parents dying are what you are dreaming. I think that the dream is something else."

"But what could it be?"

"I'm not entirely sure," she said. "Have you ever gone back to the house since then?"

"No," I replied. "I'm not even sure if the house is still there."

"How old are you, Darryl?" Dr. Pemberton asked, but I had a feeling that she wasn't expecting a response. She was merely talking through her thoughts. So, I remained silent and listened. "19? You moved when you were nine, which means that you haven't lived in the house in about 10 years. And you haven't been back there. The night terrors started about three weeks ago. Why? Why now? After 10 years? Something triggered memories buried deep in you and your mind is being a bitch about it, excuse my language, instead of simply telling you what it needs you to know."

I waited.

"Do you remember anything happening right before the nightmares began?" she asked. "Something big? Important?"

"Trista."

"What about her?"

"She told me that she was pregnant."

Dr. Pemberton nodded, as if something might have clicked.

"Now you see why I need this to stop. What can I do to fix it?" I asked, my voice becoming shaky. "Please. Help me."

"I am going to ask you to do something for me," Dr. Pemberton insisted. "It might sound strange, but I think it may help you unlock whatever memories are trying to get through."

"I will do whatever it takes," I said.

"I want you to find your old house," she began, "and if it is still there, I want you to go there. Even if the house is gone, I want you to still go to where it used to be. I think being there will be the most effective way of figuring out what is going on inside your head. Will you do that? And then come back and see me, immediately."

"If you think that it might end this torture," I said. "My Grammy should know if the house still exists."

***

After leaving the office of my psychologist, I didn't waste any time. I was desperate and finally had a possible resolution in my sight. Like a sleepy bullet, I shot from the office and drove directly to my Grammy's house. I had to keep moving. I had to keep the momentum going, because if I stopped, I may not have the energy to start back up. Something in the back of my mind told me that Dr. Pemberton was right. There was more to my night terror than just bad dreams, and I needed to find the answer.

After knocking lightly on Grammy Eustace's front door, I let myself in. Once inside the home, a long-lost memory washed over me like a warm ocean wave. At first, it was filled with forgotten emotions. Sadness. An overwhelming feeling of loss. And the total devastation of having just lost both of my parents in a single blow. I was a tiny, broken little boy walking into my Grammy's house. I wasn't there to visit or stay the night, like it had been every other time before. I was there for good. My entire life had changed, and I was helpless to do anything about it. But then, when my Grammy hugged me tight, I felt her love warming me from the inside out.

I would be okay.

Or so I thought.

I went straight to the living room and found my Grammy's tiny form sitting in the same comfortable chair that I had earlier remembered, her television set on some show that appeared to be as old as her. Grammy had her head slumped to the side and looked like she had been dozing toward a nap. I immediately felt somewhat guilty for rousing her, but she didn't seem to mind the visit.

At least, not at first.

"Darryl?" she greeted in her light voice. "I wasn't expecting you. Come in. Sit down for a spell. How are you, dear?"

I told her that I was good, before giving her a quick hug and sitting down on the worn loveseat a few feet away. The look on her face was easy to read. Concern. She knew that I was lying. She knew that I wasn't good. And I was just too damned tired to fake it.

"You haven't been sleeping," Grammy said. It was not a question. It was a fact that she could see a mile away.

"I need to talk to you about something, Grammy," I replied.

"Talk to me about what, dear?"

"About my parents," I answered, my hands trembling.

My Grammy and I had never discussed what happened to them. It was like a black spot in our lives that we purposefully never filled in with color. I can't be sure whose choice it had been, but part of me believed that, a long time ago, we both had silently agreed to never discuss it. But I needed to break that unspoken agreement. It was time. I was ready. Or I hoped I was, anyway.

"Lovely people," Grammy replied. "What about them, dear?"

"I want to talk about the house I grew up in," I said. "The house where... they died."

"Why would you want to do that, dear?" she responded. She then slowly rose to her feet and asked, "Would you like something to eat? You look like you haven't eaten in days. How about I whip you up some leftovers? I got some meatloaf in the fridge, and I can heat it up real quick."

"No, Grammy!" I responded, a little too sternly. "I need to know."

Gradually, she lowered herself back down into her chair. After a minute of silence, all Grammy said was, "It is best to leave sleeping dogs to lie, dear."

"This dog has been asleep long enough," I replied. And then I asked the million-dollar question. "Why did he do it?"

"I don't know."

"Please, don't lie."

"I'm not lying," Grammy said. "I don't know, because no one does. It was all random and evil. A horrible mess. And I don't want to talk about it. I don't want to remember them like that. My daughter. Your father. And I don't want you to, either."

"What about the house?"

"What about it?"

"Where was it?" I asked. "And is it still there?"

"You are not going there!" she said.

Her response told me everything. The house still existed.

"Please," I begged. "Just tell me where it is."

I had never seen my Grammy anything but docile and loving, but her face changed into something else. She was tortured. I was dredging up pain that she had buried long ago, and I hated myself for it.

"Mills Hollow," she mumbled. "Pennsylvania. Union Road. A pile of shit in a piss town!"

I didn't recognize the name of the town, but we were a stone's throw from the PA border.

"And the house is still there?"

"*Yes.*"

"Does anyone live there?"

"No," Grammy replied.

"How do you know?"

"Because I own the cursed thing!" she exclaimed. "And no one will ever live there again, if I have a say in it!"

"Houses don't kill people, Grammy," said.

"Don't they, though!" she replied. "If I had been smart, I would have torn the *fucking* place down years ago!"

"Why didn't you, then?"

"That house has been in our family for generations," Grammy replied and then sighed. "It has been cursed, though. Cursed and damned. And I thought that if I tore the place down, that curse would be set free to follow us here. As long as that house remains, then the curse will stay put. But now you wanna go there and stir up ghosts? So be it. Just don't bring any of them back with you."

"Thank you, Grammy," I said, rising to leave. "I'm sorry. I love you."

"I love you, too," she replied. But as I bent down to give her a goodbye hug, she latched on tight to my neck and whispered in my ear, "Wish you would let sleeping dogs to lie."

***

After packing a few things, I made a quick call to my girlfriend to let her know what was going on. I explained everything to her, and I could immediately hear the uncertainty in her voice, but she didn't try to stop me.

She knew it was important. She trusted my judgment.

Mills Hollow was a little over two hours away, according to my GPS. That meant that I should make it there before nightfall, unless a traffic issue or car malfunction slowed me down or stopped me along the way. I was putting myself in fate's hands. Fate would decide whether or not I got to where I was going, in one piece or several.

Most of the drive, especially once I got into the less populated areas, went by in a haze of worry and fatigue. Even the songs that I played from my phone began to blur into one long guitar riff and drum solo. Physically, I was directing my car down the road, but mentally, I was in a whole other place entirely.

That was until I passed a small green road sign.

Mills Hollow 10 miles.

I began to feel pins and needles at the back of my neck, at the tip-top of my spine, which intensified the closer I came to the Pennsylvania town. A familiarity set in. I knew that stretch of road. And I knew what I would find before I got there, even if it only came to me in fractured images and sensations.

Worn houses and double-wide trailers, with broken-down vehicles, doghouses, and roaming chickens filling the front yards.

A dirty General Store with a row of gas pumps out front that hadn't worked in decades. They sold freshly made subs in the back. My dad would sometimes get me a small one with turkey lunch meat, American cheese, and a glob of mayo, hold the vegetables.

An ice cream shop that desperately wanted to be a Dairy Queen. But their chocolate cones were never as good.

And at the center of town was a large, two-story school building. A million images filled my mind when I saw it. Along with a million voices. Teachers and friends. Riding the bus every morning and every afternoon. Sounds and sights that had slipped my mind long ago.

Mills Hollow was a slow country town. As I drove through it after years of being gone, my fractured memories were right in front of me in flesh and blood. And, somehow, everything seemed the same as it had been when I was a child.

The sun was on the horizon, and it would be night before I knew it. A nervousness hit, nearly causing me to find the motel I knew would be on the edge of town and hunker down for the night.

What I had come to do could wait until morning?

Right?

Wrong.

I needed to stay the course.

The only way to the other side was through.

I had quit paying attention to my GPS miles before and I didn't hear its fake female voice telling me to take a right onto Union Road, because I knew exactly where I was going.

The address of my old house was Mills Hollow, but it wasn't within the main borders of the town. Instead, it was a mile or so away from everything else. All by itself.

In the middle of the woods. As I knew that it would be. The few memories that I had of the place involved being constantly surrounded by trees. The nights must have been quiet and eerie. But, for a kid, I'm sure that there were endless shadows to explore.

The driveway to the house began as a narrow dirt road, a bumpy dirt trail that started at Union Road and then disappeared into the dense trees. It wasn't a real road. And it didn't have a name. It was only marked by a simple mailbox at its end.

Or, at least, it used to.

When I found the narrow dirt road, I pulled over and stopped instead of turning onto it. I sat idle for a few minutes and stared at the spot where my childhood mailbox used to sit. It was long gone. Not even a wooden pole to mark where it once had been. It was lost in time, like everything else. But I could still picture it. It was a tiny replica of the house that I would find at the other end of the dirt road. It wasn't an exact mimic, but it was close enough. My dad had made it himself, I remembered, and he was quite proud of his work. He hadn't always been handy, but he had his moments.

Like when he built the cellar into the tall hill.

After school, when the weather was nice, I had been allowed to ride my little bicycle to the mailbox and grab the mail. It wasn't all that far, to be honest, from the house to the mailbox, but for a little boy, it felt like I had been on an adventure far from home.

With so many memories suddenly coming to light, I couldn't help but be overwhelmed. And a little sad. The last days at my old house had been forever tragic and traumatizing, a time that I would have done anything to forget forever. However, in forgetting the bad moments, I had also allowed myself to forget the happy ones.

Coming back to my old home was forcing me to combat both, the happy and sad, the light and the dark. I just had to hope that I was strong enough.

I took my eyes away from where the mailbox had once been and let them follow along the dirt road. The sun was gone, ducked down behind the horizon. The last glow of the day was quickly fading, making it impossible to see through the darkened woods. My old house was somewhere; back behind the trees. I just couldn't see it. Yet. I could almost envision it as a living creature, lurking just out of view.

It knew that I had returned, and it was waiting for me.

I sat for another minute before finally taking a deep breath and turning onto the bumpy path that would lead me back home.

***

The dirt road was shorter than I remembered and the house at the end of it was a lot smaller. My headlights fell against the front of the structure. The few memories that I have held onto over the years painted the house, in my mind at least, as being large. Not giant. But a much larger space than I was pulling up to.

Maybe it was the way the shadows twisted beneath the beams of my headlights that made it seem smaller than it was?

Or maybe that was childhood?

Remembering things to be much larger than they were?

As I parked my vehicle, my headlights spilled overtop the building. The first impression that I got from my former home was… old. It was a single-story wooden cabin originally built back when things were created to last for generations. It had a simple wooden porch attached to the front, which appeared to be fully intact. A few modifications over the centuries, indoor plumbing and whatnot, had been made to keep the aged building in livable condition.

As I sat there staring, I couldn't deny the place's beauty, like I was looking at something from a history book.

That old cabin could have spoken a million stories. I wondered whether or not mine would be the darkest of them.

No wonder my Grammy could never bring herself to tear it down.

Yet, I couldn't help but to feel like something was hiding beneath the beauty, something sinister just below the surface. But what? That was what I was there to find out, I told myself.

A thousand memories began to unfold in front of me, phantom figures of a young child playing on the porch, running through the trees, swinging on a tire that no longer existed, like a thousand little ghosts before my eyes.

After shaking away the ghostly memories, I killed the car's engine, and everything fell into darkness. I snatched a black LED flashlight from the center console and cut the darkness with a bright new beam. Using the beam to guide me, I got out and moved around the back of my car to the trunk, which I had opened with the push of a button. From the opened truck, I pulled out my hiking pack, which I had stuffed full before leaving earlier that day.

I have always loved to hike and camp in the woods. I felt comfortable in nature. Looking around me, at the cabin in the middle of the woods, it was easy to see the possible source.

I threw the pack over my shoulder, closed the trunk, and then walked toward the cabin, up the rickety porch steps, and to the front door. Until that moment, I never thought to question whether or not I would need a key to get into the place. Luckily for me, the front door was unlocked, and it pushed open without a problem.

I didn't go inside right away. I couldn't. I couldn't say how many minutes I stood there and stared through the open doorway unable to move. My heart was pounding. My throat was tight. The hairs on my arms stood straight up. When a cold breeze brushed my neck, I nearly turned around and ran away. Back to my car. Back to the road. Back to my real home. But I didn't. I eventually gathered the courage to break the threshold and go inside.

I can't say exactly what I was expecting to find.

An empty cabin in the middle of nowhere seemed like a prime target for vagrants to hunker down or teenagers looking to party away from town. But, as I washed the area with a beam of light, I couldn't see any signs of it. There weren't any broken beer bottles, or sleeping gear, or trash, or any hint at all that anyone had been inside the place for a long time. Only a thick layer of dust and dirt.

For a brief moment, I wished that I had brought some sort of weapon. A handgun. Or a rifle. Something for protection. But it was too late, and I wasn't leaving to get one. I would have to make do with the bear deterrent spray in my pack, even though it was a few years old and might not work anymore.

From the look of it, the inside of the cabin had been cleaned out long ago. No furniture. No rugs on the floor. No hanging pictures on the walls. Nothing had remained of the family that had once called the place home. As I walked into the living area, I was greeted by emptiness and even more ghosts.

In the middle of the room, I dropped my pack with a loud *thud*. Suddenly, small dark forms began to rush by my feet. I jumped back and cried out, nearly stumbling over my fear and the empty air. Quickly, I threw the beam of the flashlight across the floor to see several tiny mice rushing from the nearby fireplace and out through the front door.

"Holy shit," I exhaled, watching the last little mouse flee from the cabin. Once I was sure there were no mice left, I slammed the front door closed. Turning from that door, my flashlight fell on another closed door several feet away. Before I knew what I was doing, I moved over to stand in front of it.

My parents' bedroom.

Boom!

Boom!

Boom!

I could not see through the closed door, but I recognized the voices of my parents reaching out to me through time and memory. That horrifying night was beginning to tear through the blockage in my mind that had been built up over the years. I had been there that night, standing right outside of the door, standing exactly where I was standing a decade later.

I had been a little boy about to lose everything.

But why?

I could hear the anger, my memory replaying the moment, and I could feel the flames that were filling the closed room. It wasn't the beginning of an argument. The argument had been raging for some time and was nearing its peak. The pressure was building and building, the momentum growing, and there was nothing I could do to stop it. It had already happened. And once the pressure finally reached its breaking point, my life changed forever.

The blockage didn't completely break up, though, and the voices were muffled. What had they been fighting about? I couldn't remember. I *needed* to remember. Desperately, I tried to listen closely to the voices, decipher words, any words, so that I may remember what was said that night.

But it remained gobbled.

Indiscernible.

I thought about breaking through the closed door. But I didn't. Because I didn't that night, either. I never went into my parents' room, that night or any night after.

The emotions in the room drastically shifted, like I knew they would. I remembered when the shift happened. The fiery anger became cold fear, at least for my mother. My father was still aflame, but my mother's voice became pleading and afraid. She was scared. As she should have been.

For a fleeting moment, both voices fell away and there was only silence. I remember how that silence felt. It was worse than the noise and yelling. That silence said more than anything else. Sometimes silence can do that, speak louder than screaming.

When the silence finally broke, it was my mother pleading for her life. I didn't have to recall the words to understand what was happening. Her voice had been shrill but hopeless. She was begging. Yet, she knew that her pleas would get her nowhere.

Boom! Boom!

Boom!

The blasts of the shotgun rattled me, even though I knew they were coming.

Two for her.

One for himself.

Like the young boy I had been, my knees gave out, and I stumbled back against the nearest wall. I fell to a sitting position and began to hug my knees. I didn't cry. Either time. I simply hid my face and wished it had all been a dream.

I don't know how long I sat there before finally getting back to my feet. I considered going into the bedroom. Would there still be blood on the walls or the floor? Had it been cleaned or merely sealed up like a tomb?

I didn't go in, though.

Instead, I recovered my pack and found my old bedroom. Both Dr. Pemberton and Grammy were right. Coming back to my house had awakened the sleeping dog. And somewhere within my memories would be the source of my night terror. Even though Dr. Pemberton had only wanted me to visit my old home, I had other plans.

I was going to spend the night.

***

There was no point in starting a fire before settling in, because the night was warm enough to suit my needs. The fireplace's flue was probably rusted shut or something, anyway. Besides. I was not worried too much about comfort. If being comfortable was a priority, I wouldn't be anywhere within 100 hundred miles of that cabin of nightmares.

After entering my old bedroom, I doused my overly bright flashlight and pulled the electric lantern from my pack. I placed it on the floor and switched it on. The light of the lantern was dimmer than the flashlight, but it would work better for sleeping. I could use no light at all, but I wasn't going to sleep in total darkness. I just wasn't.

My old bedroom was just as empty as the rest of the house. The basketball posters that I had mentioned to Dr. Pemberton were long gone, most likely having been thrown away. As was my old bed, along with any other furniture I might have had back then. The room had been gutted of everything but four walls, a floor, and a ceiling. It was like I had never been there at all. Like the room has always been empty and will remain empty forever.

It didn't matter.

I didn't need a bed.

I picked a random spot in the middle of the floor to roll out my blue sleeping mat. Once the mat was out and flat, I removed my sleeping bag from my pack as well. I made a quick bed that would do fine for the night.

I considered eating something from the various snacks that I had brought, but decided against it. Rather than put food in my stomach, I tossed back one of the sleeping pills that Dr. Pemberton had prescribed to me. I used a quick drink from a bottle of water to wash it down.

It wouldn't be long.

Without changing my soiled clothes, I slid into my sleeping bag and closed my eyes.

It wouldn't be long.

I don't remember falling asleep, but the next thing I knew, I was being jolted awake. No. Not awake. When I felt the bed beneath me, I knew that I was waking into a dream. No. Not a dream. Into my nightmare. The realization of the dream faded at the sound of movement, and the dream fully took me.

Scratch.
Scrape.
Shuffle.

I was not alone in the dark room.

Mom?

Dad?

The overwhelming smell of rotting flesh and sweat gagged me, but I fought the urge to puke. Frightened by the rancid odor, the stench of something dead, I tried to hide my eight-year-old body beneath a multi-colored comforter. There was something foul in my room and it wasn't my parents. I could still hear it moving. Closer. And closer. I could even hear it breathing. But if I hid out of sight, whatever was there would eventually go away.

Right?

But I knew better.

I peeked. Just a little. But enough to see the monster standing over me. All I could see was its head, at first, and its crooked face. Large, black eyes. Bald scalp, except for a few puffs or strands across its scalp. Its face was gaunt and covered in sickly gray skin. It saw me peeking, and it smiled. Its grin was filled with brown, jagged teeth. On its breath was the worst stink I had ever encountered.

Once again, I swallowed the urge to vomit.

My heart pounding and my breath locked in my lungs, I attempted to pull the comforter back over my face, but the monster reached out and grabbed it before I could. I struggled, but it was much stronger than me. I fought and fought, but the monster managed to pull my comforter from me and from the bed entirely.

I kicked and struck out when it tried to get its long fingers on me. I tried my best to hit whatever parts of its thin, naked form I could. However, my short arms and short legs did little to fend off such a creature. It appeared skinny, but its long arms were just too strong.

When I eventually found myself in its clutches, I remembered that I had a voice.

"Mom! Dad!" I would have yelled, if I had only remembered my voice a moment before. By the time I tried to call out, the monster was stuffing my mouth with one of my dirty socks that had been lying around the room.

There was no spitting it out.

It had been lodged in much too far.

I was on the verge of choking when the monster plucked me from my bed. I continued kicking and punching, but still to no avail. I was helpless. As if I were nothing but a lifeless doll, it bound my hands and feet with rope that appeared from nowhere. And then it stuffed me into the large feed sack that had been lying at its feet before slinging me over its shoulder. It then began to carry me away. I couldn't see clearly through the sack, so I didn't know exactly in which direction it was taking me, or how it was able to travel through my house without waking my parents, but I somehow knew what the destination would be.

The cellar out back.

***

After hearing the rusty hinges of the cellar door groan, I was bombarded with earthy smells emanating from the hole in the hill. I never liked the smell of that cellar. It was always overbearing to my nose, a strong, damp mixture of ripe potatoes, dirt, dust, and possibly mildew hidden in the cracks and crevices of the wood.

I often imagined that it was how being buried alive smelled.

The creature took me all the way to the back of the cellar before dumping me onto the flimsy wooden floor.

I fell with a hard thud and immediately tried to scurry away from the beast. I was already up against the rear wall, however, and didn't get far. Frantically, my eyes darted from one side of the cellar to the other. The walls were lined with wooden shelves and produce. The walking space was a narrow path between the shelves. Even if my feet were free, there would be no getting around the creature, who stood smack dab in the middle of the room.

I had nowhere to go.

I put my back against the wood of the rear wall and glared up at the monster. I was bound and gagged and helpless to its whims.

I could see the drool at the corner of its mouth. I could see the hunger blazing in its eyes. And I was overcome with a sense of déjà vu. I couldn't shake the feeling that everything had happened before. And that it will all happen again... and again.

A cycle.

Unbreakable.

I watched the creature grin as it came for me. Brown teeth and foul breath. It couldn't wait another minute. Out of instinct, I squirmed and tried to fight back, but I knew it would sink its claws into me either way. And when it clutched both of my upper arms to lift me from the floor, its nails punctured deep into my flesh. I howled. But my pain only spread the monster's grin wider.

Faster than I thought the creature was capable, its face lunged toward mine and bit into the soft meat of my left cheek. It bit down hard, pushing its filthy teeth all the way through into my own mouth. A dam was broken, and blood began to rush in, across my tongue and down my throat, causing me to choke and gag. Once its jaws were clenched tight, it tore the skin from my face.

I screamed, spraying blood and bits of flesh.

The agony ripping through my face blurred my vision, but I could still see clearly enough to watch the creature chew.

It loved the taste of me.

While the monster was lost in the ecstasy of my flavor, I lifted my bound legs and planted my feet against its chest. I pushed with all my strength. Slick blood had spilled down my left shoulder and upper arm, weakening the monster's grip there. When I pushed, it couldn't keep hold, and I was able to fall free.

I tumbled back to the floor, but was somehow able to get to my feet. My bindings were… gone? How? I didn't question it for more than a second. Instead, I glared at the monster, my eyes filled with hatred. If I didn't do something, it would eat the rest of me, too.

A cycle.

Repeating over and over.

No.

Something was different that time.

I was fighting back.

I stood straight, my shoulders high, and I howled at the monster who wanted to eat me. My gag was gone, too? Ignoring my surprise, I howled from my frightened gut and then spat a wad of blood at the creature's face.

"No more!" I screamed. "You will not eat me anymore!"

The monster's eyes shot open wide and the joy on its face fell away. It also knew that the cycle had changed.

"You can't do this anymore!" I yelled. "*Dad*!"

The monster began to spasm, its sickly skin trembled and quivering as its shape changed. Its claws retracted. Its teeth straightened. Its eyes went from black to green. It was still tall and lanky, but no longer was there a ravenous monster standing in front of me, but my own father.

And he looked defeated. I had taken away his power.

Suddenly, my eight-year-old body transformed, as well, into the man that I became. Grown. Strong. Ready to face the truth of my dreams. Ready to sleep soundly once more.

"You are done doing this to me," I told him, right before my dream began to dissolve.

***

I woke with a start and a gasp, climbing back to consciousness in the same place I had fallen from it. My old bedroom. Through a nearby window, I could see that the sun was beginning to rise. Somehow, the nightmare had lasted all night. I kicked away my sleeping bag and lunged to my feet. I rushed from the room and returned to my parents' bedroom door.

Memories assaulted my mind, and I started hearing their voices again, traveling to me from a time before. However, instead of muffled emotions and noise, I could finally hear them clearly and the truth I had finally faced became as concrete as flesh and blood.

"You're a monster!" my mom shouted, heartbreak filling her throat. "I saw you! I caught you! How could you do that to our son? Our boy?"

"Don't look at me like that!" my dad replied. "I am not that! I am not! Don't you dare call me that!"

"How many times? How many? *How many times did you take my child to the cellar?* I'm a monster too! I should have stopped it! I should have known! I should have stopped *you*!"

"Stop talking to me like that! I will stop! I promise! You can't tell anyone! You can't!"

"Liar! You will never stop! You can't! I will never let you near my son again! Get out of my way!"

"Where are you going!"

"I'm taking Darryl far away from *you*!"

"You are not taking my son anywhere! You hear me! You will not take him from me! Get away from the door!"

"Don't touch me! Let me go!"

"I won't let you do this!"

"..."

"..."

"..."

"Put that down." Her voice got quiet. "Please. We can talk about this. Let me leave and we can talk about this. I promise."

"*I am not a monster.*"

"Please…"

Boom! Boom!

Boom!

It had taken two shotgun blasts to kill my mother and a single blow to the head to end my father. I stood there for a few more seconds as the gunfire echoed in my brain. Then, as it eventually faded, I left that cabin, without grabbing a thing from it. Not my pack. Not my lantern. Nothing. I wanted nothing from it.

Tucked away in the trunk of my car, I always kept a bottle of lighter fluid and a pack of matches, just in case the firewood was too wet, or I simply didn't want to spend hours getting a campfire going.

It didn't take much. The cabin was more than willing to burn. And so was the cellar. And as I drove away from the blaze, I felt lighter, freed from a hefty burden I hadn't fully realized, one that had haunted me for too long.

I was free.

Free from my past.
And free from the monsters.

THE DEVIL DOWN BELOW

"THE DEVIL COMES for bad little children, Luke. He waits under their bed for them to fall asleep and then grabs their little feet. He grabs their little feet, and he drags them down below… down under the bed and all the way to Hell… where bad little children will burn in a lake of fire, forever and forever."

I heard my momma's voice that morning, in my head, as I walked up the field toward the little garden in the back 10. My little sister, Lila, stayed a couple of feet behind me. She was skipping. Her tiny feet bounced through the tall grass.

"Light as feathers," my momma always said about Lila.

The night was coming, but the sun was still up. The day was a hot one, but luckily, there was a cool wind blowing through the field. I walked slower than I should have. I wanted to feel the wind on my face. It dried my sweat. It felt mighty good.

Lila was trying to talk to me. Her voice sounded like fast gibberish and insect chirps, because all I could hear were my momma's warnings.

"The Devil comes for little children who are bad… and drags them down below."

My momma always tells me things like that, things that should scare me and make me wanna be a good boy. I ain't no dummy, though. I am smarter than she thinks, and I know that those things, devils and angels, Heaven and Hell, are nothing but pretend. They are made up. Fake. And I don't know why people ever believe in such nonsense.

But I pretend, too.

I go to church every Sunday morning, and I sit next to momma. Sometimes my Pa comes too. Sometimes he don't. Like a good little boy, I follow along in the Good Book and I stay awake whenever Preacher Wilson talks a little too long about nothing at all. I stand when Preacher says to stand. I sit when Preacher says sit. And I sing whatever he tells me to sing.

I pretend that I believe in their stories. I am sad when Sodom and Gomorrah turn to fire and ash. I praise Jesus when the Messiah cures the blind and raises the dead. And I am scared about the end of days and all the craziness that the world will see at the end of all things. I fake all of that so that my momma thinks that I am a good boy.

But that is all pretend, like I said. Because I ain't no good boy. Never a day in my life. I don't wanna be a good boy. No. That ain't true. It is not that I don't ever wanna be good, I just know that I am bad.

I just do bad things, sometimes.

I drank a beer once, when my Momma and Pa were sleeping. I took it up on the hill and drank it as fast as I could. It made me feel funny, but in a good way. I threw up. But that's fine.

I cheated on a history test in school. Someone stole the answers from the teacher, and I bought one with $3 that I took from Momma's purse. Momma just thought the money fell out of her purse sometime and never made a big fuss over it.

I found a bird once with a broken wing. It was easy to catch because it couldn't fly away. I bashed its head against a tree and watched its little brains spill out everywhere. I started plucking all of its feathers off, but then I changed my mind. I was going to make a fire and cook it, but I was already bored, so I threw it into the bush and went back home.

I can't say why, but three days ago, walking up the long field, on my way to the garden, Momma's voice bothered me more than any time before. I heard it over and over, like it would never leave me be. It would never give me a bit of peace.

"The Devil comes for little children who are bad..."

But that can't be true. The Devil never came for me. And sometimes, I did those bad things just to see if Momma's Devil was under my bed to drag me down below. But he never was.

Yet.

I could hear Lila start humming something to herself when we got within sight of the back 10 and the little garden. It sounded like a hymn from church. She was always humming hymns, like Momma. *Amazing Grace. Old Rugged Cross. How Great Thou Art. Nothing but the Blood...* Momma's favorite.

Momma's garden wasn't ever much to look at, a square patch of dirt with a rickety wire fence around it. But it is my Momma's pride and joy. She likes to grow enough tomatoes, carrots, green peppers, corn, and green beans, so that we can eat them freely when they are growing and still have a bunch to can for the winter.

Momma loves to can her vegetables. Almost as much as she loves her church and her Jesus. And she spends hours and hours in the spring and summer tending to her garden.

There have been a bunch of jackrabbits this season, though, that have found my momma's garden. Pa ain't built the fence tall enough or deep enough in the dirt to keep them out of the vegetables. And once jackrabbits are let in, they never leave peacefully. They are like tiny demons.

That evening, Pa sent me up to the garden with a rifle to get rid of some jackrabbits for him. He was too tired and seven cans deep into the beer or he would have gone done it himself. I was fine doing it for him. Wasn't the first time I killed some jackrabbits.

I love to kill the little bastards when I can.

When Lila and I got as close as I needed to the garden, I stopped, and I told Lila to stop, too, and shut her mouth. I didn't need her skipping about or her humming scaring away any jackrabbits that might be feasting on our momma's pride and joy.

I told Lila to stay put, and I started walking slowly toward the garden. I raised my .22 rifle to get it ready, just in case any jackrabbits spotted me and tried to run. I was aiming the rifle at the garden, watching for any jackrabbits that might be running around between the cornstalks, when I looked back at Lila to make sure she had stayed way back, like I told her.

It looked like the sun was sitting right on top of her shoulders. The light was shining right on top of her body. It was like she was glowing. Like the Lord Jesus was shining his light right on top of her.

If you believed in him, anyway.

My sis was three years younger than me and, as my momma said, she was an angel on earth. Long, wavy blond hair. Bright blue eyes. Flawless skin. Perfect grin. She brightened up the world.

"Angels are a gift from the Lord Jesus. They are part of him on this earth and they are given to us to make our lives better. They lift us up when we have fallen. They brighten all that is dark in our world. And when we die; they take us up to Heaven to be with Lord Jesus, forever and forever."

And, right then, I swear that she looked like an angel to me, too. Where I was bad, I knew, right then, that my sister was good.

Lila was the only one to ever hug our momma when she cried. I always seemed to make momma cry even harder.

Lila was the only one who could make our Pa smile. I always seemed to make him madder and fussier than a rattlesnake.

As far as I know, Lila never stole, cheated, or hurt a fly.

I heard something moving in the garden. I looked away from Lila and back down the sights of my rifle. I could see the fur of a Jackrabbit going for the rows of carrots. Little bastard wouldn't be eating a single damned one.

I followed it with the tip of my rifle and waited for the little bastard to stop moving. I could see its little ears bobbing up and down and its little butt moving all around on the ground. I held my breath for nearly a minute, because I didn't want the Jackrabbit to hear me breathing. When it stopped to take a bite of carrot, I fired two fast shots. And then I ran to the garden and hopped the rickety fence.

One shot missed.

But one shot hit the bastard right through its hind end. Put a hold clean through. When I got to it, I could see it trying to drag itself away. Its back leg wouldn't work. It was making a trail of blood through the dirt. I stood for a short bit and watched it crawl. Its eyes got real wide when it saw me, but it couldn't crawl fast enough to get away.

I dropped the rifle and grabbed it up by its neck. I could have shot it again, but I didn't. I grabbed its neck tight with both my hands and I squeezed. You would think a jackrabbit had a weak neck, but it don't.

I had to squeeze real hard.

And I didn't know jackrabbits scream.

But as I choked it to death, its eyes wide and popping out its head, it screamed louder than any person I knew could. It sounded like a little girl dying. The harder I squeezed, the louder it screamed.

Until the bones snapped.

I had done forgotten about Lila. I had been too busy killing. But then, when the jackrabbit died, I heard my sister start screaming. She had watched me kill with my hands. She knew that I liked it. And she saw that I was being bad.

The little angel.

Eyes full of fear and tears.

She was afraid of me.

I heard my momma's voice again in my head.

"Angels are a gift from the Lord Jesus."

I don't remember dropping the dead jackrabbit or picking up the rifle from the dirt.

"The Devil comes for little children who are bad."

I sighted the rifle on Lila and thought about what would happen if I were to kill an angel of the Lord Jesus. What could be more bad than that? The Devil would have to come for me. Right? And if he ain't coming to get me for it, then none of it's real. Like I said all along. It's all pretend. Stories.

I fired.

Lila stopped screaming.

A bit of blood shot out from her neck, and she fell down like a sack of wet dirt. I dropped the rifle again and ran over to her. Bright red blood was pouring from her neck where there was a large hole. Lila wanted to talk, but her voice would never work again. No more gibberish or insect chirping. No more humming hymns.

I got down in the tall grass next to her and watched her life empty onto the ground. There was a glow in her eyes, like fire. And I almost believed in church. But the fire went out. She didn't grow wings and fly away, like an angel. No angel came down to lift her to Heaven, either.

She… just… died.

I looked up into the sky and silently challenged the Lord Jesus. Come take your angel! Smite me for being bad! Smite me for killing your light! If you are real! Do it!

But he never did.

I told my momma and Pa that it had been an accident. I ain't meant for it to happen. Lila spooked me and the rifle shot by mistake. I ain't mean for it to happen. I swore. But Lila got hit in the neck and there was nothing that I could do to keep her from bleeding and dying. It was too fast.

We buried Lila this morning.

I made Momma cry more than I ever have before. She won't leave her room. I can still hear her crying through the walls.

I don't know how many cans of beer my Pa has drunk today, but it's way more than I've ever seen. He went into the woods a while ago. He couldn't walk all that straight. He took the shotgun. I don't know where he was going or when he will be back.

They still love me, but they hate me, too. I don't know if they believe me about Lila. I think they might know that I am bad now.

I am in bed, and I just can't sleep. The sun is gone, and my room is black. I can't see anything at all. If Lila was light, then I guess I am the other thing.

Darkness.

Something is under my bed, moving around. It tries to be quiet, but I can hear it scratching the wood of my floor. I don't know what it is. And I'm afraid to get down and look. Maybe a jackrabbit has gotten in. One never has before. Maybe one has. But I never heard a jackrabbit hiss like this.

Or maybe I am wrong.

If I look, maybe I will see the red eyes of the Devil. If I get too close to the edge of my bed, maybe his red hand will grab me. He will sink his black nails into me and drag me down below, where I will burn in a lake of fire, forever and forever.

Maybe.

I curl up in the middle of the bed and think about praying. But I don't. There is no use in it now. I uncurl my body. I put my feet over the side of the bed and wonder if the Devil will take me down below.

Will he come for me?

How could he not?

After what I have done?

I put my feet to the floor, and I waited.

JUPITER STREET

Sun has set on Jupiter Street
and the hounds are closing in
Their howls are all around me now
warm breath upon my skin

Ever so swift with my escape
and still they found my scent
Vicious gnashing drives me deep
into this dark descent

I am a good man
into the night my plea
But no one's there to hear my lie
except the hungry hounds and me

The path that led me to this hell
is again beneath my feet
A plain stretch of patient road
simple concrete and deceit

Orbs from streetlights guide me
like dim halos on the ground
Against the odds I find my home

terrified of what might be found

A single light in the window
A single door in the way
A single fear of what's beyond
as my guilt screams stay away

I am a good man
calling out another plea
like myself and the hungry hounds
the closed door will not believe

The nails of hounds drag and scratch
sudden growls close to my back
I hear their tongues eager and wet
anticipating their attack

With a primal desire to taste my meat
and feed on my fragile skin
the beasts made chase back to my home
but I'll be damned if I don't get in

Twisting the knob I cry her name
and through the open door I flee
I drastically seek forgiveness
from my beautiful Austin Lee

But an awaiting nightmare then returns
of betrayal that devoured whole
my only love with someone else
entwined with another soul

A loaded gun appears to me
insanity in my hands
first the other before my love

and then the final bullet lands

Even a good man can be damned
losing the only love that he has known
for when a man is eaten down
he is left with nothing but bare bone

And I am a good man
a lie no one will believe
not myself nor the hungry hounds
nor my Austin Lee…

… Sun has set on Jupiter Street
and the hounds are closing in
Their howls are all around me now
warm breath nearly upon my skin

AWAKE INTO A DREAM

JOSEPH KEPPT WAS suddenly overcome with a sense of loss, which caused him to lose track of what he had been doing. He paused for a moment, because the emotion was deep and unexpected. Everything else sank and seemed to vanish into this newly opened, previously unseen abyss.

Leaning back in his leather chair, Joseph tried to shake away the unexplained sadness. He focused on the groan of the chair as it moaned beneath his weight. The creaking of the joints and the shuddering of stretching leather were familiar sounds.

The sensation of loss was not real, Joseph knew. It was a river without a source. He could build a dam, but there was nothing to dam up. He could not block a phantom stream.

Joseph loved his life. Everything about it. And his brain had simply made a mistake. Released the wrong chemical? Misfired the wrong neuron? He could not say for sure.

What am I about to do, Joseph asked himself.

Looking around, Joseph tried to gain some grounding. It was a desperate swim for dry land after being plunged into the phantom river. The familiar wooden walls of his home office enclosed him. Beneath him was the same old dark carpeted floor. And above him was the same old dark-colored ceiling. A short leather sofa sat against the far wall. Family pictures hung within cedar frames.

Same old, same old. Everything was where Joseph had left it. Safe and secure.

The leather chair groaned again as Joseph leaned forward. Returning his fingers to the keyboard of his black laptop, Joseph squinted to read the words that filled the monitor.

I had been writing, he reminded himself.

Joseph had begun working on his third novel and was about to place the final paragraph of Chapter Eight. Quickly skimming over the last couple of sentences, he attempted re-entry into the fictional world from which had been abruptly pulled away.

His third was very special to Joseph. With the success of his first two works, *The Uneven Sunlight* and *The Mouse in the Kitchen*, Joseph had earned more freedom with the recent artistic endeavor. He was able to relax and have fun with it. The pressure was still present, but it no longer felt as if two worlds, the real and the imaginary, were resting upon his shoulders.

Also, the early stages of a new story always seemed to excite Joseph. The exploration into a fresh and uncharted reality was electrifying, filling his mind with sensations unmatched by nearly everything.

As he finished reading the last words written, Joseph was quickly able to jump back onto his initial train of thought. He began to type. *Tap. Tap. Tap.*

When Benji woke, he immediately knew that the explosion had taken his leg. The absence was unmistakable. Yet Benji did not rise from his bed in a frantic search for his missing limb. Instead, he rose, pain pulsing through him, and began to scan the hospital room for Crystal. Was she there? And when his eyes met hers, he knew that she was and always would be.

The antique clock on the wall behind Joseph's head began to chime nine slow, melodic pulses. 9 pm. *I am supposed to do something at 9 o'clock*, Joseph told himself. *But what?*

Kimberly.

Her bedtime story.

Joseph glared at the new paragraph for several seconds before saving them. He always hated walking away from an unfolding work, but he would happily do it for his daughter.

For a moment, Joseph tried to recall how long he had been writing. He wasn't sure. He couldn't even remember exactly what time he had begun. Yet, he knew he had been working for a while. He had eight nearly finished chapters to prove it.

Glancing to the title at the top left corner of the screen, Joseph murmured aloud, "*A Walk for Crystal*, I shall return to thee."

Rising, Joseph briskly exited his office.

✻✻✻

Kimberly was already buried beneath her light blue comforter when Joseph entered the room, her hair still slightly wet from her nighttime bath.

"You ready for bed, kiddo?" Joseph asked.

"Yep," Kimberly replied, her face lighting up because she knew what was about to happen.

"Brush your face and wash your teeth?"

Kimberly giggled.

"Brush my teeth and wash my face, silly," she replied.

Joseph watched his daughter closely, each muscle as they flexed to form her gentle smile. Innocence. That was what Joseph saw when he looked at Kimberly. And possibilities. Like a blank page. The potential was infinite.

"Oh. Okay. Did you?"

"Yep," Kimberly replied, squirming into a position deeper below her comforter. "Why am I going to bed so early and you and mom don't have to?"

"You know you have to go to school tomorrow, kiddo," Joseph reminded his daughter.

"I know. But why?"

"If you get up early and go to school every day," Joseph began, "you will get real smart and then you can become a lawyer or doctor."

"Really?"

"Yep," Joseph replied. "And if you don't go to school every day, the best job that you can hope for is becoming a circus midget."

Kimberly giggled again.

"What if I don't want to be a doctor or a lawyer?"

"You don't?" Joseph asked, with a curious tilt of his mouth.

"No," Kimberly replied.

"Really?"

"Yeah," Kimberly replied. "I want to tell stories, like you, dad."

"You still have to go to school to tell stories," Joseph informed her, sudden pride filling his face. "Every day."

"Really?"

"Yep," Joseph said. "I went to school each and every day, whether I wanted to or not."

"You did?"

"Yep," Joseph lied again.

"Okay."

"*Okay*," Joseph copied. "Now, until you are old enough to tuck *me* in and tell *me* a bedtime story, how about I continue *The Tale of Kimberly, the Elvin Princess*?"

"Okay."

Joseph walked over to the side of Kimberly's bed and sat down on the edge. She readjusted her body, giving her father some room. Leaning forward, Joseph clicked off the lamp on the small bedside table. The room was suddenly engulfed by an empty black, which immediately activated the sensor in a nearby nightlight. A light red light filled the black with color.

A light red light?

When did I buy Kimberly a red night light? Her nightlights have always been yellow, Joseph told himself. And yet, there it was. Strange. Maybe Catharine bought it?

For another second, Joseph let himself ponder the existence of the red light, which, for whatever reason, reminded him of strawberries.

"Kim the Elvin Princess rode hard," Joseph began. "She drew closer and closer to the edge of the Black Forest. Kim could see Witch Tower on the horizon, rising over the Wandering Trees. Twisted. Spiraling into the clouds. Robert, prince of the gnomes, was near. Kim knew it in her heart. She would rescue him from Gertrude the Green, and they would marry. Like the Oracle had predicted. It was fate. It was destiny."

Joseph continued on, listening as his daughter's breathing became deeper and steadier with each word. He spoke on and on until the rough sound of Kimberly's first snore stopped him.

Rising slowly, Joseph gently kissed Kimberly's forehead, trying not to wake her. "Love you, kiddo," he whispered. "Forever and ever."

***

As he headed back toward his office, Joseph noticed a slight glow coming from the master bedroom. Instead of turning right and heading back to his writing, Joseph made a sharp left.

"Busted," Joseph blurted, as he leaned against the frame of the open doorway.

As Catharine glanced up from the novel she was curled up with, the low lamp lit her face and caused her green eyes to glimmer. The cover of the paperback was fully exposed to Joseph, the muscular, bare-chested man peering out at him, giving him a sexy wink.

"This isn't what it looks like," Catharine replied, a small smirk perking her lips.

The phantom loss briefly returned. It touched Joseph's neck hairs like a cold breeze and then retreated.

"How could you?" Joseph asked. "If my peers found out that my wife reads drug-store-romance-novels, I would be ruined."

"Honey," Catharine said, pretending to grovel, "I can explain."

"I would be shunned from the literary community. Blackballed by any decent publisher. The only thing I would be allowed to write is corny children's novels. *Everyone Poops 5: Still going*." Joseph closed the door and began to slowly make his way toward the bed.

"Well," Catharine replied. "If you would perform your husbandly duties, then I would not have to read this smut."

"First you betray me professionally?" Joseph began, moving a few steps closer. "Then you degrade me sexually?"

"Pretty much."

Joseph reached the bottom of their king-sized bed.

"I have no choice then."

Joseph crawled onto the bed. With both hands, he felt his way along Catharine's leg, which was covered by loose pajama bottoms.

"What are you doing?" Catharine followed the question with a burst of laughter. "Cut it out!"

"I have to end you to save my dignity," Joseph replied. Reaching Catharine's midsection, he raised the bottom of her t-shirt to reveal her belly button. "I am sorry, my love." Putting his lips to her stomach, Joseph violently blew, making his lip and her skin vibrate.

Catharine exploded. Grabbing her husband, she guided his face to hers, until their lips met. They made love fast, then slow, and then fast again, never turning off the small lamp. Every motion was like the steps of a well-rehearsed dance, fluid and in sync. Years of practice and dedication had created the perfect rhythm.

Afterward, Joseph rolled over, exhausted. Sleep was coming, and he was content to have it. He was not leaving, simply resting. Everything and everyone he loved would still be there when he woke.

Safe and secure.

Joseph dove into the void, doing a swan dive into sleep.

***

Joseph Keppt woke with a gasp, as if finding breath for the first time in years.

Before opening his eyes, he reached over to feel the warm skin of his wife. However, he found nothing but empty air. He reached further, and then further still, his hand searching for Catharine.

He never found her.

With a jolt, Joseph rose. Every joint in his back and arms ached, as if the space between his bones had been filled with rough sand. But he didn't care about the pain. Where was Catherine? Was his wife somewhere near?

"Catharine?"

As he rapidly peered around the small room, he knew that she wasn't. It felt as if his whole reality quivered, shivering with the chill of total confusion.

Searching the room around him, Joseph tried to find familiarity to support him, to give him solid ground. But the room was not familiar. It was not the same one in which he had fallen asleep. The alien environment forced Joseph to remain free-floating in chaos and bewilderment.

A faint red light touched the darkness of the strange room, layering everything with the color of strawberries. The red was coming from a small night light next to the bed.

Joseph let his adjusting eyes scan the area. There was a simple wooden dresser sitting off to the left. A foot or two from the dresser, he could make out what appeared to be an opened bathroom door. A black television hung from the wall opposite his bed, held by an extended metal arm. In the far-right corner of the room, he could see a large off-white door.

While the bedroom that he shared with his wife had been filled with love and happiness, the strange, alien room he stared into felt empty.

Dead.

Joseph's heart sped up.

His chest began to hurt.

"Catharine?" Even his voice seemed different. Full of grit. "Catharine?"

Joseph threw the thick blanket aside. He saw that he was wearing blue plaid pajamas.

But I had fallen asleep naked. Hadn't I?

Joseph pulled his legs out from the blanket, before slipping from the bed. Quickly, he walked to the off-white door. He tried the knob. It wouldn't turn. Locked. Had he turned hard enough? He tried the knob again. Still locked.

The door had a small window, shaped like a lopsided rectangle. Joseph twisted his neck. This way. That way. Trying to see through the tiny window. A faint fluorescent light. An empty white wall. He couldn't see anything else.

"Hello?" He began to shout. "Hello?"

He pounded his fist off the door. It hurt. He hit again, anyway. Again. And again.

"Is anyone out there?"

Joseph yelled.

"Can anyone hear me?"

Joseph pounded.

"Help me!"

Was he trapped in a dream? A nightmare? Or had he died in his sleep? Was he in hell? Imprisonment for all eternity? No one that he loved with him? All alone?

Through the window, off to the right, he saw movement. It was subtle, but Joseph was sure that it had been real.

A shadow.

A figure.

He couldn't be sure.

"Help! Help me!"

Someone suddenly came down the hall to the door, but the details of them were blurred to Joseph. He took a step back from the door. Another step. And another. From outside the door, Joseph heard a buzz, followed by the sound of the lock disengaging. He readied himself. Planting his feet, he was prepared for whoever was to come into the room.

Friend or foe.

The door slowly opened inward.

Joseph's breathing increased, keeping pace with his heart.

A short, middle-aged woman entered. Her shirt was colorful, and her expression was that of shock and subtle confusion.

"Mr. Keppt?" She asked, masking her confusion with sincerity. "You shouldn't be up and about at this late hour. Let me help you back into bed."

"Who are you?" Joseph asked, backing away as the woman approached.

The woman paused.

"Who are you? Where am I?"

"Please," she replied. "It is late. And you need your rest." The woman managed to place a hand on Joseph's arm. "Let's get you back into bed. A good night's sleep will do you beautifully."

"Get your hands off me!" Using his palm, Joseph pushed the woman backward, nearly causing her to stumble to the ground.

"Calm down," the woman replied. "There is no need to get angry."

"Where is Catharine!?" Joseph screamed. "Where is my wife!?"

"There is no need to scream," the woman replied. "Everything is alright. Everything is okay."

"Nothing is okay," Joseph said, coming closer to the woman. "Where is my wife? Where is my daughter? What have you done to them? Why are you keeping me here? Where the hell *is here*? I want answers! *Now*!"

"Calm down, please."

"I will not!"

Suddenly, Joseph sprang forward and shoved the woman again, causing her to lose her footing and tumble to the floor. Upon seeing his own outburst of violence, Joseph fled. Into the open bathroom, he hurried, slamming the door shut behind him.

Total blackness fell over him like a shroud.

"What do you want from me!?"

There was no answer.

"What do you want!?"

His voice became weak, desperate, scared.

"What do you want!?"

At first, the dark around Joseph refused to deteriorate. His eyes refused to filter it and the black remained impenetrable, empty, blank, like an ebony page, unused. Instead of words, Joseph filled the void with images. Catharine's face. Her body. Naked. As it had been when he last saw her. Smooth skin. Tanned. Flawless.

Gone.

The loneliest word in the English language.

Joseph could no longer feel Catharine nearby. Her scent had vanished. The connection had been lost. He could not feel her. The absence was unmistakable.

Gone.

Somewhere inside him, the word rang true.

Gone.

Joseph's eyes somehow focused on the faint strawberry light that spilled in from beneath the bottom of the door, revealing faint shapes around him. A toilet. A sink. A tub. A mirror.

"Mr. Keppt," a male voice said. "Mr. Keppt. My name is Doctor Ramone. I believe that I have some answers for you. If you would please come out and join me."

"No!"

"What happened?" Dr. Ramone said, seemingly asking the middle-aged lady who must have been nearby. "What triggered this?"

"I don't know," the woman responded.

"Well, something did," Dr. Ramone replied.

Without noticing the motion, Joseph found himself sitting on the seat of the toilet.

"I know you must be frightened, Mr. Keppt," Dr. Ramone spoke. "It is completely reasonable. And understandable. But, if you come out here, we can talk about it. We can sit down, face to face, and I can try to explain everything. Do you understand? Mr. Keppt? Mr. Keppt? Do you understand what I am telling you?"

"Where am I?" Joseph chose not to raise his voice, because the fight was quickly draining from him, filling the toilet bowl beneath him.

"Please come out of the bathroom, Mr. Keppt," Dr. Ramone pleaded.

"Where am I?"

Joseph could feel the doctor's frustration, like sound waves pulsing through the walls.

"*Blissful Wanderings*," Dr. Ramone finally answered. "A resting home for…"

"Why?"

"Why what?"

"Why are you keeping me here?"

"You are," Dr. Ramone began, "very ill, Joseph. We are not keeping you here. You are a patient here."

"You're lying."

"It's the truth," Dr. Ramone replied. "Please come out. I would like to speak to you and not the side of the door."

"You will tell me. You will tell me." Joseph's hands began to quiver uncontrollably.

"Dementia."

"Dementia?"

"For over 20 years," Dr. Ramone clarified. "I can't explain what is going on right now. You have been catatonic. Barely responsive for almost a decade. You haven't spoken more than a couple of words in years. And now. This."

"You're lying."

"What is the last thing you remember?" Dr. Ramone asked.

"My wife. My daughter. Being at home. Writing. Going to sleep in my own bed. Strawberries."

"What year?"

"2019."

Silence.

"2019!"

"It's 2050, Mr. Keppt," Dr. Ramone replied.

Again, without feeling the motion, Joseph found himself standing. The small bathroom seemed even smaller, somehow claustrophobic. If he had room, Joseph knew that he would pace side to side, end to end.

2050?

Impossible.

Wasn't it?

"Mr. Keppt?" Dr. Ramone seemed to be growing even more anxious. "Did you hear what I said?"

"Yes," Joseph answered. "I don't believe you."

"I am not trying to deceive you in any way," Dr. Ramone began. "I know how it must sound. I know how hard it must be to swallow. But I insist that you try. You are not yourself, right now…"

"I am myself. I know myself," Joseph replied. "And I know how to spot lies. I know how to spot stories and fairy tales. I write them for a living. I create fiction, and I can smell bullshit a mile short of Texas."

"Just listen to me please," Dr. Ramone begged. "You are not well. Your mind is not well. You cannot trust yourself. Do me a favor, *Joseph*. Look in the mirror. But brace yourself."

Joseph's entire body paused, blood and heart and breath. No. No. No.

"Prove me wrong," Dr. Ramone insisted.

The mirror was two steps away. Joseph inhaled. One step. And then exhaled. Another step. A dark figure met him there. Barely a shadow. Hunched. Faded.

Who is that? Joseph asked himself.

Turning at the hip, Joseph found the light switch. The fluorescent bulbs overhead flickered a few times before springing fully to life. Suddenly, fully revealed by the light, an old man, wrinkled and worn, glared back at Joseph from within the looking glass.

A stranger with a familiar face.

Joseph quickly closed his eyes.

That is not me.

"Where is Catharine?" Joseph asked the question again, still hoping for some sort of response.

"Your wife…" Dr. Ramone began. "Catharine passed… nearly 6 years ago."

"And my daughter?"

"I don't know," Dr. Ramone replied. "*We* don't know. No one has been able to contact her for several years. She signed your care completely over to Blissful Wanderings, full decision-making ability, and then disappeared."

"Am I dead?" Joseph asked, squeezing his eyelids tighter.

"No. You are very much alive."

"Is this damnation?"

"No. This is illness."

"Is this even real?"

"Yes. Everything you are experiencing is 100 percent real."

"Am I dreaming still? Have I not woken yet?"

Joseph opened his eyes. The old man was still there.

"You are not me," Joseph told the old man, watching the old man's lips move in the same manner. Was the old man mocking him?

"What was that, Joseph?" Dr. Ramone asked. "I couldn't hear you."

"You are not me," Joseph repeated, watching the old man's eyebrows twitch. He watched the old man very closely. He watched for differences, inconsistencies in movement.

"You are not me. My wife is asleep next to me, her arm across my chest. My daughter is in her bed down the hall, dreaming of fairy tales and horses. My wife is not dead. My daughter is not gone. Not gone!"

The old man's nostrils flared. *My nose did not flare*, Joseph told himself. *His nose flared. But mine did not. Right?*

"You are not me!" Folding his fingers, Joseph slammed the base of his two fists into the mirror. He was shocked when they did not simply pass through. "Come out of there!" He struck the mirror again. And again. Fractures erupted and spread. Shards of glass began to rain into the sink. Another hit. And another. The pieces continued to fall, as did the drops of maroon blood.

Sleep to wake, Joseph thought, remembering the nightmares he had when he was a child. He would run.

He would fight. But the monsters never stopped, until he finally decided to give up, to fall down, to play dead. That was when he would wake up. Only then would the nightmare end.

Taking a large sliver of broken glass, Joseph held it to his wrist. "Sleep unto death, and wake into dream," he said, quoting one of his favorite poems. He then cut, making a deep slice, starting at his wrist, and then going down his forearm. He watched his skin split. "Dream unto life, and sleep forevermore."

"Get this door open now!" he heard Dr. Ramone shouting, but the voice grew further and further away.

The bathroom spun. The blood flowed. And Joseph did not fight to remain conscious. He would let sleep take him. Hope made it easy. Hope that this cold reality would no longer be. In his bed, safe and secure, he would return.

Joseph allowed his body to fall to the tile. The blood was like the light, peeking under the door.

Red.

Like strawberries.

***

"And the wedding was grand. Everyone traveled far to attend, from elf to gnome to pixie to posie. The sight of true love and destiny brought them all together. As Kim and Robert kissed, their first kiss as husband and wife, there was no doubt that their ending would be happy, no matter which road they rode down next. No evil witch nor troll king could separate them, because love would always bring them back to each other. The end."

As Joseph finally finished his fairy tale, he knew that Kimberly had been asleep for several minutes, and that he would have to just finish it again the next night. But that was okay. Joseph never minded a re-write, because it only made a good story even better. He wished that life worked that way.

"Love ya, kiddo," Joseph said, slowly brushing Kimberly's forehead with his lips. "Forever and ever."

Joseph gently rose, trying not to stir his daughter's peace. Walking towards the door, heel to toe, trying to be silent, Joseph paused.

When did Kimberly's night light become red? He wondered. *Did I buy that? Or did Catharine?* It reminded him of something.

Not blood.

Not wine.

Strawberries…

SHACKLED AND CHAINED

THE DARKNESS CONFUSED him.

Gabe couldn't remember losing consciousness, yet he was regaining it. Wherever he had existed, prior to waking up, must have been an empty void, black and nothing else, because there was no memory of it, not even a fleeting, dissolving dream. And the moment that he reentered the world from whatever dreamless sleep had somehow taken him; questions immediately bombarded his mind.

Where was he? How did he get there?

After managing to slide open a pair of heavy eyelids, Gabe realized that he was in a dark room, one consisting of stone and earth. It was less of a room and more of a cave with gray rock walls and a dirt floor. The oval cave was maybe 20 yards around, give or take a yard, and a single source of light fell into the room through the window of a wooden door.

Gabe peered over at the door. It was quite large and built into the stone wall on the opposite side of the cave. It was dark red and appeared thick and solid. The window in the door was a small rectangle through which a column of yellow light poured. There didn't appear to be any glass in the window, only a row of horizontal steel bars. The door seemed not to have a knob or handle of any kind, either, at least not on his side of it.

The light shining through the horizontal bars wasn't solid, like from an electrical bulb, but fluid, as if from a flame of some sort.

"Hello?" Gabe called out weakly.

None of it made any sense. It was like rousing from sleep, only to find yourself entering into a nightmare.

"Hello?" he said again, not entirely sure if he expected an answer.

What made even less sense was the fact that he was not lying down or standing up, but instead, he was kneeling, his knees planted against the dirt floor.

There was a heavy chill that filled the cave and seeped down deep into him. The cold poured into Gabe's muscles and filled his bones, making him tremble. Struggling to move his shaking body, Gabe slowly climbed to his feet. The effort left him winded and with a swirling head, but he managed to stay upright.

Both of his arms hung down in front of him, bound together at their wrists by a pair of medieval-style metal shackles. The shackles were connected to a thick steel chain. Gabe twisted around and followed the chain to find that it was connected to the stone wall behind him.

"Fuck!"

Taking several steps toward the wooden door, Gabe pulled the thick chain until it was taut, and he couldn't pull it any further. He then yanked as hard as he could. Once. Twice. There was no use. The chain was not coming free of the wall.

Giving the chain one final, frantic yank, Gabe pulled as hard as he could. A sharp, tearing pain carved its way through the muscles of his shoulders and forced a guttural scream from his lungs. The scream echoed against the rocks and multiplied into a macabre chorus of pain and fear.

He was a prisoner. But how? Why?

Gabe tried to remember, but found his thoughts fractured. He attempted to focus, but it was difficult to think clearly.

What was the last thing he recalled? Where had he been before waking up?

The baby…

The baby…

***

Like a confused, annoying rooster, the baby was awake again and screaming before the sun even began to peak out from the horizon. Before the day even began to shine, Gabe's precious baby boy was filling the two-story home with the loudest screeching a small body could produce, making sure that both of his parents were fully awake along with him.

And Gabe *was* fully awake, whether he wanted to be or not.

He knew that once the crying began, it wouldn't stop for a very long time. It didn't matter if the baby was fed and clean and should otherwise be content, because nothing seemed to make the boy happy or quiet.

The screeching would go on. And on.

Gabe stood in the doorway of the master bedroom, dressed in black sweatpants and a black t-shirt. For a minute or two, he silently watched his wife as she desperately tried to comfort their child.

Shelly. Blonde. She was still technically young, but the last couple of months had aged her immensely. A white nightgown clung to a thick body that had once been thin and tight. Giving birth to their little bundle of joy had taken a toll on her perky form, stretched skin and ugly scars had taken over her once flawless flesh.

"I'm going to take the dog for a run," Gabe told her, knowing that the need for a run had nothing to do with the dog.

"I'm going to try giving our son a warm bath," she replied, giving him the usual glare.

But Gabe ignored it and turned away.

The crying was like sharp daggers to his brain, and he needed to get out of the house or risk losing even more of his sanity. A run alongside the ocean might clear away the screaming from his mind and give him a chance to regret his life choices. Gabe had never wanted a wife or a child, but he accidentally fell into both.

Everything just happened so fast, too fast for him to have corrected the course or halted it altogether. And mistakes are like snowballs, as long as they keep rolling, they only get bigger.

Leaving them behind, Gabe rushed downstairs to retrieve the dog.

Their dog, Roscoe, was a hyperactive pom and was always up for going outside. And it didn't take much convincing to get the little guy on board. With the little dog circling his ankles, Gabe rushed out of the back door and into the cool air. The chill instantly felt good against his skin, creating goosebumps along his arms and at the back of his neck. It gave him a little more energy and he could feel his mind beginning to clear already.

A long and narrow stretch of empty beach, where swimmers and surfers and even boaters were forbidden, sat several yards from the rear of the house. Gabe broke into a steady jog as soon as his sneakers hit the sand. He always enjoyed the emptiness and isolation of that stretch of beach, because he could be all alone with his thoughts.

Hopefully, the gentle waves beating against the shore could soothe him.

But then Roscoe barked…

Not barked…

The little dog howled at something further up the beach…

But what…?

***

Gabe tried to hold on to the memory, but a sharp pain struck his mind and shattered his thoughts like a rock hitting weakened glass. Something had happened on that beach. He needed to remember what. He knew that the memory was important, yet whenever he tried to reconstruct the events, another surge of pain broke it apart again.

Images of Shelly and their child that morning lit up in his mind like flashbang grenades, bright and vivid but at the same time agonizing and disorienting.

"Fuck!" he shouted to the rock walls.

The echoes cursed back at him.

Gabe slowly returned to his feet, but the act punished both his muscles and his bones. From head to toe, his body felt like it had been beaten by a large blunt force weapon, beaten so brutally that his mind had chosen to erase all memory of the attack in order to keep his sanity intact.

But who had done the deed? And where was his attacker? Gabe wanted to know, but at the same time feared the answer.

There was a spot in the far corner of the stone room, directly to the right of the wooden door, where the column of light failed to fully penetrate the darkness. Something suddenly drew Gabe's attention to that spot.

Movement. It appeared as if the shadow itself had shifted, or maybe something within the blackness had changed positions.

Maybe it was his imagination.

Or, at least, that was what Gabe was trying to convince himself of when something stepped forward from the shadowy corner. The creature was a mixture of body and smoke, gray from top to bottom, except for a pair of glowing red eyes and tattered white rags that hung off its body. Its flesh was the color of ash, and its long, wild hair was a darker shade of the same color.

The smoke was what mostly drew Gabe's attention. It was like an aura that consistently rose from the creature's body, thin puffs rising as if from a campfire, before disappearing a few inches in the air.

It was all very strange and somewhat hypnotizing to look at.

As the creature rushed across the floor, slapping the dirt with its bare feet, Gabe was struck by the stench of grime and sulfur. He jerked backward, but in a blink the gray creature was in front of him, its red eyes staring him down. It was the same height as Gabe and met him eye-to-eye. The maroon that filled the creature's eye sockets reminded Gabe of the nosebleeds he used to get as a young kid. The fresh flowing blood was always vibrant, almost neon in color.

There was hate in the creature's eyes, as well. It loathed him. Like the aura of smoke, Gabe could feel hatred emanating from every part of it.

Being that close to the creature allowed Gabe to see fissures and cracks running along and across its gray flesh. Some deep. Some shallow. Some thin. Some gaping. Like when someone drops a ceramic plate and cracks form like spiderwebs, but the plate doesn't fully break apart. There was an especially deep crack that ran down the length of the creature's face, starting from its forehead and falling to its chin.

That specific crack was so deep and profound that it seemed as if the creature had two separate faces. Within the crack, Gabe could see a deep black ooze, thick and crude like dirty oil from a car engine.

"You are here with us," the creature hissed. Its breath smelled like rot and decay. "You… will never be free… of us."

Suddenly, the creature lashed out, raking sharp, jagged fingernails across the right side of Gabe's face, tearing open four long gashes into his skin. One of the fingernails sunk clean through his cheek and into his mouth, forcing meaty chunks of flesh through the gaping wound. The pain of his face ripping open was sharp and intense. As Gabe retreated backward from the attack, his shackled hands raised in defense, the creature remained in front of him, until eventually, Gabe's back struck the rock wall of the cave.

The thud of his bareback hitting the cave wall reminded Gabe of something, something from that morning.

It wasn't the exact sound, but close…

Something…

Hitting against rocks…

✷✷✷

Gabe should have put Roscoe on a leash that morning, but while rushing from his house and his screaming child, he hadn't even considered it. And as Gabe watched the dog rush off toward whatever had grabbed the little guy's attention, high-pitched barks filling the morning air, he immediately regretted the oversight.

Roscoe was a good dog, though.

Like most small dogs, Roscoe pretended to be brave and ferocious, but in the end, would be too scared to venture very far from Gabe's protection.

20 yards or so up the beach, Gabe could faintly see his dog, who had halted at whatever had drawn him away from his owner. Gabe squinted as he jogged toward the dog, but the sun was only a thin sliver on the horizon and there wasn't enough light for him to yet see what Roscoe had found.

Joining his dog, Gabe came upon what initially appeared to be trash scattered across a large area of sand. Had someone dumped their garbage? It wasn't unheard of. But it only took him a moment to realize what the sight actually was. Large fragments of torn, twisted metal. Wooden boards, broken and scattered. Pieces of glass and plastic.

Taking his eyes from the wreckage, Gabe peered out at the stretch of ocean and the rough waves that repeatedly slapped against a multitude of sharp, jagged rocks rising in the distance. The peaks of those dangerous rocks went on for miles in all directions.

There was a reason why swimming, surfing, and boating were forbidden in that area. It was far too dangerous.

Shaking his head, Gabe had deadly scenarios play out in his mind. A boat, fishing or leisure, had come that way by accident or stupidity. Maybe they hadn't seen the danger in time. Or maybe they were too confident and arrogant to see it for what it was. Either way, once the rock had its grip on them, there would be no turning back.

No escape.

What the hell had a boat been doing out there?

As the questions plagued Gabe, a series of frantic barks from Roscoe pulled his attention back to the beach.

He couldn't immediately see the dog, but followed the barking to the other side of a large piece of contorted metal. Behind the destroyed section of the boat, Gabe found the bodies of two young men lying unexpectedly at his feet, both stiff and dead.

His hand went to his mouth to stifle a shriek.

How long had these men been there? Not long, Gabe figured, because their clothes were still somewhat damp after having been in the water for who knows how long.

The bodies of the two young men were grotesquely battered and contoured, and Gabe hoped that they had been lucky enough to drown before they were repeatedly bashed against the rocks.

Damn it!

The dog leash hadn't been the only thing he had forgotten whenever he had fled from his wonderful family. He had left his cell phone behind as well. He needed to report this to the authorities, but before he could run back for a phone, a splash of color stopped him in his tracks.

Red. Vibrant. Almost neon.

Even in the dim lighting of the still waking morning, Gabe could see the bright color, which was a great contrast to everything else. One of two men held it in his hand, grasped tightly in a firm death grip.

Stooping down, Gabe took a closer look…

And found…

And found…

***

The creature was no longer hissing.

It was screaming at Gabe, "You will not leave us! You will… not… be… free… of… us!" as it continued to claw frantically at his face, neck, and whatever other areas of flesh that it could rip open. Blood and bits of skin ran freely down his naked body.

Terrified and desperate, Gabe pressed his back into the rock wall, harder and harder, hoping that the wall would magically disappear, and he would have a way to escape this horrific entity. But the wall remained solid. And Gabe remained a prisoner.

Maybe he couldn't run, but maybe he could fight.

But how?

With his hands still shackled together?

That was when the creature unexpectedly stopped its attack and took two steps back from Gabe, creating a slight gap between them. Yet, the moment that Gabe eased his weight from off the wall, the creature lunged again and shoved him back against the rocks. The impact stole Gabe's breath and caused his legs to give out. As he crumbled downward onto one knee, Gabe both heard and felt several stones somehow coming free of the wall and falling onto the dirt floor next to him.

Acting out on instinct, Gabe grabbed for the fallen rocks. Taking the largest one into his bound hands, he leaped to his feet and charged the creature.

He struck it in the head with the rock. Once. Twice. Again. And again. He heard bones snapping beneath the onslaught.

Even when the creature fell backward and landed in the dirt, Gabe climbed on top of it and continued to pummel its head. The deep crevice that once perfectly split the length of its face fractured and grew, becoming a massive web of cracks and breaks.

Dark, crude oil spilled from the destruction and the stench of it was like nothing Gabe had ever smelled. It was putrid. Like a mixture of infection and feces. And he couldn't keep himself from vomiting. Quickly, he leaned off to the side, away from the creature's body, and released yellow and green bile into the dirt.

After he was done throwing up, his muscles still clenched tight, Gabe let out a primal scream that filled the cave with an onslaught of echoes. But even when the echoes of his own voice died away, he could still hear voices screaming.

Other people.

Other people shrieking and wailing from somewhere beyond the wooden door, other prisoners most likely trapped, shackled and chained, as he was.

As the other screams filled his cave, Gabe's eyes shifted to the large rock that he still clenched in his fist. It wasn't gray, like in the walls around him, like what should be expected. There were smears of black oil splattered across its surface, but underneath it was…

It was…

***

Bright red.

Like the blood of a freshly opened vein.

Without consciously deciding to do it, Gabe leaned down and took the strange stone from the dead man's hand. It wasn't like anything that he had ever seen before. It was an oval, almost like an egg, larger than a baseball but smaller than a football. The red of it was so bright, it was almost glowing. And the surface was smooth, nearly flawless, except for splotches of dark, wet sand and strange symbols that were carved into it.

But the red…

Like blood…

That was what kept pulling at his thoughts…

The red…

Like blood…

***

There was bright blood everywhere.

Gabe stood over the dead form of the creature that had imprisoned him, the smooth stone still clutched tight. Her head was smashed and crushed beyond recognition. Red splotches were scattered all through her yellow hair and across her white nightgown. Cracks and crevices disfigured the once young and beautiful face.

A barking dog drew his attention. Roscoe was in the room's doorway and yapping frantically. But another noise immediately grabbed Gabe away from his dog.

"You will never leave us!"

Gabe jerked his head toward the words, toward the voice, toward the small crib in the corner.

"You will never escape us!"

Walking over to the crib, Gabe peered down into it, before raising the stone high above his head.

ABOUT THE AUTHOR

After being brutally mauled by a dog as a toddler, Jackson Arthur grew up with a stutter, which caused him to be socially awkward. Instead of interacting with people, he chose to hide his nose in books, causing him to fall in love with fiction. At an early age, he began to read *Goosebumps* and *Fear Street*, before graduating to more adult novels like *The Stand* and *The Green Mile*. His love of scary stories blossomed into the desire to scare people himself.

    Jackson Arthur currently lives in Ohio with his wife, daughter, mean cat, and an old chinchilla.

Printed in Great Britain
by Amazon